First published in the United Kingdom in 2023 by Lantana Publishing Ltd.
Clavier House, 21 Fifth Road, Newbury RG14 6DN, UK
www.lantanapublishing.com | info@lantanapublishing.com

Text © Shiko Nguru, 2023
Artwork & Design © Lantana Publishing, 2023

Cover and internal illustrations by Melissa McIndoe.

The moral rights of the author and artist have been asserted.

All rights reserved. No part of this publication may be reproduced, stored in a retrieval system, or transmitted in any form or by any means, electronic, mechanical, photocopying, recording or otherwise, without the prior written permission of the copyright owner.

Paperback ISBN: 978-1-915244-40-6
PDF ISBN: 978-1-915244-41-3
ePub3 ISBN: 978-1-915244-42-0

Printed and bound in China using plant-based inks on sustainably sourced paper.

For my children,
Ella, Lamu and Tawi

You give me the strength to keep going.

Intasimi Warriors Book Two

ODWAR VS. THE SHADOW QUEEN

SHIKO NGURU

Prologue

The air was stale, thin, *cold*.

Odwar felt like he was stuck in a pitch-black freezer that reeked of mouldy bread and spoilt milk. His nose burned with every short, sharp breath.

Something stirred up ahead. Twin pairs of glowing eyes flashed at him as they zoomed by, faster than a speeding car on a deserted road.

Odwar squinted into the darkness, his skin prickling at the thought of the creatures out there. As much as he tried to make out their shapes and track their movements, he couldn't. They were formless wraiths. Wisps of shadows against a backdrop of blackness.

Hellish moans and scratchy whispers called out from every side.

He blinked.

Skreeek.

It sounded like a metal rake dragging across a chalkboard. He rubbed his eyes to gain a better view and—

Skreeek!

ODWAR VS. THE SHADOW QUEEN

It was louder now. All around him. Moving in closer every time he closed his eyes.

He blinked again.

SKREEEK!

Odwar spun around feverishly, terror mounting in his chest. Whatever was once out there, was now here. With him.

He couldn't dare blink. One more and who knew what would happen. That *thing* was already on top of him. Although he couldn't see it, he could feel its puffs of rank, icy breath blowing over his head.

He fought to keep his eyelids open. His eyes stung and watered, but he held on, struggling against the itchy, burning sensation for as long as he could. Until...

Blink.

The Bull vs. the Housekeeper

Odwar fought to hold back the yawn ballooning in his chest. He clenched his jaw, sealed his lips shut, and tried to force his body to stop drawing in air. But his lungs continued to fill up. *Loudly.* His nostrils flared and hissed like two mini hoovers, trying to suck up all the air in the room.

Hoping to muffle the sound, he raised a balled fist to his mouth and pressed it up against his nose. But that didn't work. In fact, it made things even worse. With his airways partly blocked, the hiss turned into a loud, high-pitched, nasally whistle.

He quickly dropped his hand and ping-ponged his eyes nervously between the two other people seated at the dining table that morning. With Mum being away for work, it was just three of them at breakfast: his dad, seated at the head of the table, with his brother Gor next to him on the right, and then Odwar, several empty seats away from them both.

Two sets of eyebrows — one raised in surprise, the other wrinkled in disapproval — met his darting eyes.

ODWAR VS. THE SHADOW QUEEN

And in that moment, it struck Odwar how identical the faces at that table actually were, including his own.

How they could look so similar and yet be so different baffled him. Like his dad and Gor, he had smooth, dark skin and a chiselled face, and he wore his hair in a neat fade. Like them, he had an athletic build and stood almost a foot taller than his mates. The three also shared the same magnetic personality, the kind that made them wildly popular in school, or in the case of their father, popular in the Kenyan government.

Yup, they were alike in many ways, but now, all that seemed to matter was the one thing that made Odwar different from the two of them: his newly acquired gift.

This gift had created an invisible wall, separating him from the men in his family. A wall that seemed to grow wider and taller with each passing moment. It made every situation tense, awkward, *painful*.

And so, in the room filled with dark elegant woods, surrounded by richly-coloured drapery and with a dazzling chandelier overhead, the only sounds to be heard were the clinking of metal against porcelain as the three ate in rigid silence.

Then came The Yawn.

One shrill, oxygen-sapping breath in.

One long, ear-popping breath out.

THE BULL VS. THE HOUSEKEEPER

Odwar froze.

Maybe it wasn't that loud. Maybe Dad hadn't heard. Maybe he'd be grateful the air had come out of one end and not the other.

"Do you know what yawns are?" Dad's voice boomed across the table.

Maybe not.

Odwar winced as he sank deep into the cushioned dining chair, wishing the plush velvet would swallow him whole. He knew what was coming next: one of Dad's lectures.

"I asked you a question," Dad rumbled, impatience etched into his voice.

Odwar swallowed hard on a spoonful of millet porridge.

"Y-yes, sir. Yawns are a sign of laziness," he answered. Gluing his eyes to the porridge in front of him, Odwar sighed inwardly. He'd heard his father give this particular speech more than a few times in his twelve years of life.

"Correct. They're a sign of laziness. Laziness of the mind or of the body. Which one of those are you suffering from, son?"

Dad smoothed the corners of his raven-black moustache, then planted his palms on the table and leaned forward. He turned his head to one side and pointed at his right ear, a gesture that always prompted quick replies from those it was directed at.

Odwar scrambled to think of an answer that would put an end to the scolding, or at least not make things any worse. But nothing came. Even though he had been in this situation more times than he could remember, his mind was completely blank. His friend Maina called moments of utter confusion like these brain farts, always seeming to get them when teachers called on him in class. This was Odwar's biggest brain fart of all time.

Desperate, he sent a pleading look in his brother's direction, but Gor kept his eyes fixed on the table. No surprises there. Nothing had been the same between them since Odwar had acquired the one thing Gor had wanted all his life — a superpower.

Only one of them could get it. Only one child in a generation could inherit the superpowers of their legendary ancestor, Lwanda Magere. Everyone thought it would be Gor. Even the name given to him at birth was special: Gor, named after Gor Mahia, the most powerful magician to ever live amongst the Luo people. It was the perfect name for the boy who everyone thought would be the superhero of the family.

Except, he wasn't. It was Odwar who was gifted with supernatural powers. Odwar: the younger, smaller, far-from-perfect brother.

Everything had changed once it was clear that he was the chosen one, and Gor wasn't.

There was a time when Gor, who was eighteen years old and looked like Odwar's taller twin, would have jumped to his rescue at that table. He would have come up with some way to distract Dad and ease the tension. Afterwards, when they were alone, Odwar would have thanked him, and his brother would have slapped him on the back and told him that that was what brothers were for.

But that was then. Now? Now, Gor didn't even spare him a look.

"I asked you a question," Dad said, raising his voice. "Is it your mind that's lazy or your body?"

Odwar dared to look up at him. "Neither, sir. Sorry, it won't happen again."

Father and son held eye contact for one more painful second, before the former blew out an exasperated sigh and returned to reading the newspaper in his hands.

Odwar slouched back into his seat and brooded as he gulped down almost-cold porridge. Dad was always picking on him, like it was *his* fault that fate had chosen him instead of Gor. *His* fault that he was the gifted one. *His* fault that his superpower had manifested at the same time as three other kids', something that had never happened before.

Dad had been harder on him ever since he and his friends had discovered just how special they were. All four of them were Intasimi, a word meaning magical charm. They were the chosen ones, the ones who would carry on the magical legacies of their legendary ancestors. What was more, Odwar and his friends weren't just a bunch of kids with powers. They weren't just Intasimi descendants. They were Intasimi *Warriors*, a group of kids with magical strengths who were all exactly the same age. Together, they were destined to use their powers to protect the world from evil.

None of it was his fault, and yet it seemed like Dad punished him for it every day.

He was still stewing in the unfairness of it all when the housekeeper shuffled through the large French doors that led into the dining room. She was a petite woman with tight cornrows in her hair and wore a standard black housekeeping dress with a starchy white apron tied at the waist. In her hands, she held a silver platter with Dad's porridge bowl on it. His breakfast was always the last to be served, straight from the cooker and lava-hot, just the way he liked it.

It must have been this housekeeper's first day of work

THE BULL VS. THE HOUSEKEEPER

because Odwar had never seen her before. And judging from the way her hands trembled as she gripped the dish, she had already heard about Dad's quick temper.

The other house staff called dad "The Bull". And although nobody would dare call him that to his face, Odwar found the nickname to be remarkably accurate. Just like a bull, Dad raged when he was mad, mauling everyone in sight with the brutality of his words.

Beads of sweat dribbled down the housekeeper's forehead, sliding past her lips which she licked nervously. Her approach towards the table was painfully slow while still managing to be devastatingly wobbly, like the worst possible contestant in an egg and spoon race.

Odwar noticed that the bowl she carried was far too full of porridge. She, far too nervous. There was absolutely no way she was going to stick the landing without a disastrous spill.

He watched as his father folded away his newspaper and then rapped his fingertips impatiently against the table, eyes flicking from the housekeeper's pinched face to the tray she held out in front of her.

And then it happened. She took one final, jerky step, hesitated for a brief moment and then, seeming to make the decision to get it over with as quickly as possible, lurched forward and slammed the tray onto the table.

The result was, as Odwar had predicted, a complete catastrophe. The silver dish clattered onto the table, causing the bowl atop to bounce and spin on its base. With each whirl, heavy dollops of porridge splashed into the air and landed on every surface, including all over Dad's shiny suit. After what felt like hours, the clamorous spinning mercifully came to an end, leaving behind stunned, pin-drop silence in the room. It was so quiet that when a glob of porridge dripped from Dad's nose and landed on the table with a splat, it sounded like someone had just been slapped on the cheek with a fish.

The wide-eyed confusion on Dad's face was priceless and Odwar had to purse his lips as a bubble of laughter floated up his throat. He would have burst into a fit of uncontrollable giggles if, just then, the housekeeper hadn't let out a terrified whimper and slapped a trembling hand over her mouth. Her eyes were frozen open and she was shaking like a tattered flag in a storm.

Odwar's amusement was quickly snuffed out. He knew he had to act. Dad's face was already twisting, making him look so much like a raging bull that horns were likely to sprout from his head at any moment. His chest was heaving and his porridge-smeared nose flared as he glowered at the petrified woman.

No matter what consequences might befall him,

THE BULL VS. THE HOUSEKEEPER

Odwar knew that he had to do something, *anything*, to protect this housekeeper from The Bull.

"I know where my Entasim is," he blurted out.

Dad's head snapped towards him.

That's right, Odwar thought, *focus on me*. He felt like a matador, waving a giant red cape in front of a bull. The giant red cape in this case, of course, was his Entasim — a magical object that intensified superpowers. Every Intasimi bloodline had one, and every Intasimi descendant longed to get their hands on it. The only problem was that most of these special heirlooms had been lost, stolen or destroyed over the centuries.

An Entasim was a hard thing to find, and Odwar had just lied to his father that he had all but found his.

Knowing full well that it was a dangerous thing to do, he went a step further, doubling down on the fib when he saw the housekeeper slowly start to slop up the mess she had made.

"Yeah, I figured it out," he declared, the words — no, the *lies* — rushing out of him like air out of a whoopee cushion.

"My Entasim is hidden near Kisumu town, buried inside the Kit-Mikayi rocks."

Odwar's only comfort was that this wasn't a *complete* lie. More like...a very good guess. Something that could very well be true, only he didn't have the proof that it was. *Yet*. Although he and his friends had already agreed to go on an adventure to look for his Entasim, that was not to be for several more weeks.

"Mr Lemayian thinks me and the others should go and check it out," he continued.

Now, *that* was a total lie. In fact, Mr Lemayian — the Intasimi Warriors' mentor and recently appointed school headmaster — had specifically told Odwar and his friends *not* to go out looking for any Entasim. It was too dangerous. He had warned that people who had an Entasim in their possession would do anything not to lose it, including hurting those that tried to take the prized objects away.

Odwar felt a little less guilty about the lie when the housekeeper flashed him a grateful smile before scurrying backwards out of the dining room.

"Interesting," Dad said, using a napkin to dab at the brownish-white stains on his face and suit. "Do you have any idea what it is?"

Odwar relaxed a little. The conversation was steering closer to things he could actually be truthful about. "I'm thinking that it could be a spear or...or maybe a shield?"

Both he and his father knew that the Entasim could be anything. No Intasimi descendant knew what form their family's magical heirloom would take. Only a few weeks ago, Mwikali — one of the other kid warriors — had found *her* Entasim, which had turned out to be a twisted horn. It had upped her intuitive abilities, giving her crazy spidey-senses in addition to her already cool power of being able to see into the future and the past. Odwar could only hope that *his* Entasim gave him such an amazing power boost.

"And what's your strategy? How do you intend to secure the Entasim?" Dad prodded.

Strategy? Odwar squirmed in his seat. All he had was a hunch about where the Entasim could be and a very vague idea as to how to get it.

Another brain fart. He bought time before answering by taking five consecutive gulps of porridge. "Well...first we need to plan a trip to Kisumu, of course. Then...once we get there...we...will..."

Dad silenced him with a sharp look and an even sharper click of the tongue. "You have no strategy. No plan at all. And what happens when you fail to plan?"

"You plan to fail," Odwar replied, tiredly. Did parents know how mind-numbingly boring their catchphrases were?

"And I don't tolerate failure. Come up with a plan, because you and the other Intasimi Warriors are heading to Kit-Mikayi this week, during your half term break."

Odwar's heart hammered in his chest. This had gone further than he had intended it to. He had no idea if his Entasim was actually at Kit-Mikayi.

"I don't know, Dad. I mean, it's a long trip to Kisumu... The others need time to ask for permission, and besides, they might already have plans for the break—"

"Nonsense. I'll clear it with the parents. You and your friends will leave for Kisumu the day after school closes — first thing Thursday morning. You'll head straight to Kit-Mikayi to retrieve the Entasim. I'll be in Kisumu as well so I'll meet you afterwards."

Dad pushed up from the dining table and strode towards the double doors, pausing briefly before throwing them open. "And Odwar? You better have your Entasim by the time I see you."

Half Term Monday vs. Mummy Monday

Odwar's feet begged him to stop pacing. They ached terribly from all the walking he had done through the night. Still, he continued the steady plod, dragging himself from the bedroom door to the football-adorned accent wall, over to the multi-screen gaming setup near the window, on to the adjacent bed and then back to the door. He'd completed the circuit so many times that he'd created a distinct beaten path along the carpet, all but wearing it out in the places his feet had trudged through.

While tiresome, the endless pacing had done two important things: given him a chance to come up with some sort of plan to get his Entasim and, more importantly, kept him *awake*. Away from the recurring nightmare that haunted his sleep.

He paused to rub the sleeves of his school blazer, wincing at the pain that seared up his arms where the scratchy fabric brushed his bruised skin.

That was no ordinary dream, he realised with a shudder. Ordinary dreams didn't leave you with a rotten smell in your nose and a foul taste on your tongue. They didn't leave you gasping for air. Ordinary dreams didn't leave you with scars.

When the first rays of light had finally peeked in that morning, he had welcomed them, feeling grateful for once that his parents insisted on 6am family breakfasts. He longed for some company — even his father's. Because anything was better than the terror of being left alone in the aftermath of his nightmares.

Odwar pushed past his fears and tried to focus on another problem: finding his Entasim. The plan had always been for him and his friends to go up to Kit-Mikayi one day and look for it. But first, they would do enough research to be sure that it was actually there.

Now, thanks to Dad, the trip had been bumped up to just a couple of days away, leaving them with no time to dig for information. They just had to go and hope his Entasim was buried where they suspected it might be.

The thought of what would happen to him if he failed in this mission made Odwar's stomach knot. His father would know that he had lied, and whatever punishment he received was sure to be awful. Maybe Dad would even follow through on his threats and send him to a school in a whole other city.

No, he had to succeed. And he would stick to a simple plan to do it — the only plan he had.

HALF TERM MONDAY VS. MOMMY MONDAY

Odwar pulled back the curtains, allowing the yellow morning light to pour into the room. The warmth and brightness of it, even just the knowledge of what light meant — especially to him — calmed his nerves.

He was aware of its presence even before he looked, and when he finally dropped his eyes to the floor, he smiled. His shadow had already begun to move on its own, stretching and growing as he watched it, becoming longer, then wider, and finally lifting off the ground entirely. Right there in front of him, it transformed itself into a swirling cloud of black mist.

His shadow. *That* was his magical power. A supernatural strength inherited from his ancestor, Lwanda Magere.

And although Odwar's magical shadow had only appeared months ago when his gift had emerged, it already felt like a part of him that he couldn't live without. As long as there was light, it was with him. And when he needed protection, it blew where he needed it to go, blinding anyone unlucky enough to be trapped inside its opaque fog.

He smiled as the shadow encircled him, feeling braver than he had only minutes before. Just as it was with his warrior ancestor, Odwar's shadow was his strength.

Unfortunately, his joy at seeing it was cut short by a

throbbing in his arms, a painful reminder of last night's dream. He still hadn't told anyone that he'd been having frequent nightmares. Nightmares that kept getting more vicious and...*real*.

Besides the fear of Dad sending him away to school somewhere beyond Timbuktu, the nightmares were the other reason he was desperate to find his Entasim. He hoped that the magical object — whatever it turned out to be — would make him stronger, braver, less afraid of the terror he faced at night. Maybe it would even get rid of the nightmares altogether.

Perhaps it wasn't so bad that the trip to Kit-Mikayi had been forced upon them so soon; not only had the nightmares been getting steadily worse, now they had crossed the line from spooky to downright terrifying. Now he was sure that they were *more* than just bad dreams. And he had proof.

With dread lining his stomach, he rubbed his sweaty hands against his school trousers before slowly sliding his blue blazer sleeves up to the elbows. The moment his forearms came into view, his shadow began to thrash around wildly. It was scared. And so was he.

He sucked in a breath as he took in the deep, angry scratches that raked across his skin from elbows to wrists. Scratches that weren't there when he went to sleep the night before.

Odwar jumped when a knock sounded at the door, and hurriedly covered up his arms. He knew who it was just by the softness of the sound — it was Mum, freshly returned from her trip and coming to check on him before school, like she always did. He caught a glimpse of himself in the mirror that hung on the door right before it swung open, quickly noting that his tie — coloured in the vibrant shade of Savanna Academy red — was slightly askew against his white button up.

Mum poked her head in just as he wiggled his tie into place.

"Odwar? Oh good, you're all dressed," she said approvingly. Her warm smile brightened up the room even more than the sunlight had. Mum was good at that. She could light up the world just as fast as Dad could darken it.

His parents were living proof that opposites attract. Mum was a tiny woman with bronze skin, thick, brown hair and a gentle nature. If Dad was a bull then Mum was a dove, and the only thing they had in common was their belief that the sky was the limit to their dreams. Whereas Dad funnelled all his energy into politics, Mum put hers towards the non-profit organisation she had founded.

Planting a kiss on his forehead, she drew back to

look him in the eyes. "Are you ready for your half term exams?"

He nodded, feeling confident that the hours poured into revision would be enough to ace them. However, lingering thoughts of his nightmares must still have haunted his eyes because Mum instantly quirked a doubtful eyebrow.

"I'm not buying that, kiddo. You look worried. I think what *you* need is a Mummy Monday to get rid of your half term blues," she declared, squeezing his shoulders. "Get your stuff, I'm dropping you at school today."

"YES!" Odwar beamed as he pumped his fist. He couldn't grab his backpack and dash to the car fast enough.

Mum laughed as he launched his bag into the backseat and then threw himself bum-first into the passenger side.

"I'm thinking street food breakfast followed by some drive-through shopping. Sound good?" she asked as they drove down the long drive. The car paused briefly for the security guard to open the massive metal gate before easing onto the road.

Odwar's head bobbed up and down in excitement.

Mum had first introduced Mummy Mondays on the first day of nursery after seeing how terrified he was to go

HALF TERM MONDAY VS. MOMMY MONDAY

to school.

"You can't be sad on Mummy Monday," she had soothed. "That's when we get to do a bunch of fun stuff before school! It's the most special day of all!"

On Mummy Mondays, he and Mum broke all the rules on the way to the school drop off: they blasted music from the car speakers at ear-splitting volume, stopped by their favourite kibanda restaurant for the best street food that Nairobi had to offer, and then shopped in traffic for random bits and bobs from street hawkers, all before screeching into the school car park just in time for the morning bell.

"Here we go!" Mum squealed, cranking up the volume in the car. She sang along loudly to Fally Ipupa's smooth voice, presently crooning from the speakers. Having learned French in school and after spending a lot of time working in French-speaking Africa, Mum was fluent. She sounded like she could have been one of the Congolese musician's back-up singers. And even though Odwar didn't understand a word of the language, he couldn't help but join in, swaying as he played an imaginary guitar on his lap.

Their car turned into a side street and slowed down outside "Mwenda's Kibanda". The sweet smoky smell of roasting sausages was enough to make Odwar's mouth drip with anticipation.

"Four smokie pasuas please!" Mum called out to the man standing behind the grill. It was barely seven in the morning and they were likely to be his first customers of the day. He gave them a grateful thumbs up before getting to work on their order.

With speed that only a street food expert could manage, he snatched a freshly barbecued sausage off the grill and ran a knife right down its plump middle. Then, he scooped up a heaping of diced tomatoes, onions and coriander and stuffed it into the crease of the cut, only stopping when the sausage was dangerously close to bursting with filling. Finally, he squeezed lemon, sprinkled salt and dribbled hot sauce all over his pink tube-shaped masterpiece. He repeated the same preparation three more times, each time at a more astonishing pace than the last.

And so, in less time than it took Mum to turn off the engine and rifle through her handbag for her wallet, Mwenda was proudly thrusting the sizzling smokie pasuas into Odwar's ready hands.

"Best. Smokies. Ever," Odwar raved through a full mouth as the booming car wound its way back to the main road.

"Agreed!" Mum laughed, licking sauce from

the corners of her mouth. "Next up, drive-through shopping!"

The street vendors of Nairobi were a familiar sight on the city's roads. Shoals of them drifted in and out of traffic and along pavements selling everything from live rabbits to flip-flops. Odwar and his mum took turns closing their eyes and then buying the first thing they saw when they popped them open.

Odwar went first and roared with laughter when he ended up with an alphabet chart for toddlers. Mum's turn got her a decent painting of two Maasai women. They were both satisfied when Odwar landed on a pair of colourful socks and even more delighted when Mum's go won them a packet of potato crisps.

"Dad would die if he saw us eating these," Odwar pointed out, palming a handful of greasy crisps into his mouth. "Did you know he's convinced that these are fried in *electrical transformer* oil?"

Mum snorted. "It's probably what makes them so yummy," she joked.

When their giggling died down, Odwar sighed and crumpled up the empty crisp packet. "I wish he was more like you," he said quietly.

She turned down the music volume and slowed down as they neared the Savanna Academy school gate. "He's more like *you* than you know," she answered, throwing him a sidelong glance.

Odwar clenched his jaw and stared hard out of the window, craning his neck as far as he could so she wouldn't see the hot tears that burned in his eyes. "I'm nothing like him," he choked out through the lump in his throat.

They drove in silence the rest of the way, and then, with the car parked and the engine off, Mum used a single finger to turn his face back to her. "Do you know how you were named?"

Odwar blinked the tears out of his eyes and combed through his memory for the answer. "A month after I was born, my grandmother, Dana, massaged me with coconut oil, shaved my head and then announced my name during my naming ceremony."

"That's right," Mum confirmed. "As is tradition among our people, you got your name one month after you were born, in the presence of the whole family. Names are very important in our culture — like a chapter in history that tells a little bit about the events or emotions surrounding the baby's birth."

"Gor got his name because he was born the year the Gor Mahia arena was built," Odwar remembered.

"Right again. And you were named Odwar, from the

HALF TERM MONDAY VS. MOMMY MONDAY

verb 'to want, need, *yearn* for'. It was your dad *not* your grandmother who picked out your name. He insisted on it. He said that all he had ever wanted, more than anything in the world, was a last-born son."

She unlocked the car doors and turned the engine back on. "I'll have a discussion with your father about bettering your relationship...but...I want you to know that there's a world of meaning poured into the names we give our children, Odwar. Never forget that."

ODWAR VS. THE SHADOW QUEEN

Keeping Secrets vs. Telling Lies

"My life is over," Mwikali said dramatically, dropping her head onto the book that lay in front of her. It was a thick Swahili revision text whose pages, although new, bore the dog ears and creases of a book that had been used for decades rather than a mere few months. "There's no way I'm ready for this exam. No. Freaking. *Way!*" she squeaked into the open book.

Odwar heard her all the way from the doorway of the Grade 6 classroom and chuckled.

Mwikali had only moved to Kenya a few months before and was always worried about her grasp of the Swahili language, even though — thanks to hours of hard work — she could speak it almost fluently now.

She, Soni and Xirsi were at their desks which were, as they had been for some time now, bunched together to form a square at the back of the classroom.

"You'll be fine," Odwar said, sliding into the chair beside Xirsi's. "You've been practising day and night for months now. You know more Swahili than some kids who've lived here their whole lives!"

Mwikali's afro floated off the desk like a big, fluffy cloud as she rose and spun around to face him. The red highlights that weaved through her full crown of hair seemed to blaze brighter than ever under the full glare of the room's fluorescent lighting. An equally bright glimmer of hope twinkled in her eyes as she looked at him. "You really think so?"

"I *know* so. And besides, English is up first, so you still have time to study for Swahili later. Xirsi can even give you some extra tutoring over the break. Right, bro?" Odwar asked, tipping his head to the side.

"Yup, and then tomorrow you can return the favour by helping me study for ICT," said Xirsi, whose name was pronounced *Hersi*, flashing his signature lopsided smile. Xirsi's honey-brown cheeks were smeared with jam and margarine, evidence of the half-eaten sandwich in his hand. He was perched on top of his desk, swinging his legs gleefully as he finished off his breakfast. An impressive layer of breadcrumbs covered his uniform, all the way from the collar of his white school shirt to the hem of his navy school shorts. "We can head straight to the library as soon as we're done here," he concluded, before hopping off the desk and circling around to take his seat.

Mwikali chewed on her lower lip and then nodded,

KEEPING SECRETS VS. TELLING LIES

even managing a smile before wheeling back around. "Thanks guys," she said, returning to her study of the textbook determinedly.

Left facing Mwikali's back, Odwar couldn't ignore the stab of guilt that pierced his heart. That bit about studying with Xirsi in between tests wasn't just a helpful suggestion for Mwikali's benefit, it was part of a plan he had hatched the night before. A plan to keep his friends too busy and distracted to notice that he was being haunted by terrifying nightmares.

Out of all his friends, Mwikali was the one he needed to avoid most of all. As a Seer — of both the future and past — she was likely to sense that something was wrong with him a lot quicker than the others. There was no telling how soon she would figure out that something weird and quite possibly evil was going on with him.

Odwar did plan on telling his friends about the nightmares...eventually. But for now, he had chosen to keep the secret to himself, partly because he wanted to understand what was happening to him, but mostly because of the shame he felt at being so terrified. He felt bad about hiding the truth. Mum had told him once that keeping secrets was sometimes the same as telling lies. And in that moment, the idea that he was doing either of those things made Odwar feel sick to his stomach.

All the same, the first part of his plan had worked perfectly. True to his word, Xirsi looped his arm through Mwikali's and led her out of class as soon as their first exam was over. Odwar watched with a satisfied smile as Xirsi's curly mop of brownish hair bounced alongside Mwikali's red-streaked one until they both disappeared among the throng of kids headed to the library.

The smile was still pasted on his face when a blast of pain suddenly exploded up his arm. He buckled over, cradling his arm against his chest. Soni jumped back, startled. Unknown to her, she had just squeezed Odwar in the exact spot of raw skin where he had been scratched the night before.

"Geez, are you okay?" she asked, nose crinkled.

Odwar bit down on the pain, grinding his teeth together to keep from crying out. All he could manage was a nod as he covered up his wince with a shaky smile. Soni's puzzled eyebrows remained pulled together as she watched him slowly unbend his hunched body. But when he took a boxer's stance and threw some playful air jabs, the tension in her face relaxed.

"Have you been working out? You almost broke my arm!" he teased.

"Haha, very funny," she smiled, waggling her head. "But actually, I *could* use a workout. Should we go to the field?"

It was time for the second part of his plan. He had banked on Soni asking him to do some superpower practice during the breaks between exams. More than the others, she was always trying to perfect her abilities, always trying to squeeze in sparring sessions when she could. A study break between exams was exactly the kind of opportunity she wouldn't want to pass up.

Odwar knew exactly what to say to distract her. "Aren't you signing up for the Mashujaa Day dance?"

Soni's eyebrows shot up. "The what?"

He pushed on, encouraged by the spark ignited in her eyes. "On Wednesday — Mashujaa Day — we're not just dressing up as Kenyan heroes; there's going to be some sort of dance festival in the field as well. It's open to anyone who wants to perform. There's a sign-up sheet in the Prefects' Lounge and everything."

Soni was in a full-blown sprint out of the classroom even before he got the last word out.

The final portion of his plan had gone off without a hitch. As a prefect, Odwar knew that the school was always looking for ways to spice up national holidays, so he had texted a suggestion to the head prefect: instead of simply dressing up as legendary heroes, or Mashujaas, as they always did, why not add to the day's excitement by putting on a series of dance performances too? The head prefect had jumped on the idea, as had their headmaster, Mr Lemayian. Arrangements were quickly made for a sign-up sheet to be placed in the lounge first thing that morning. Naturally, Soni was going to sign up because the only thing she loved more than becoming a better Intasimi Warrior was dancing.

And just like that, his plan was complete. Mwikali and Xirsi would be study buddies over both exam days, while Soni would be fully caught up rehearsing for the dance event. In this way, Odwar was able to escape the notice of his friends for the first two days of the week. And by the time Wednesday, the last day of school, rolled around, the excitement surrounding the Mashujaa Day dance festival was all anyone could talk about.

As always, the friends came dressed up as their own legendary Intasimi ancestors. For Odwar, Soni and Xirsi, who had known of their special bloodlines since birth, it was a long-standing tradition. Mashujaa Day was the day they got to wear costumes and pretend to be the great Kenyan heroes they were descended from. This year, Mwikali would get to join in the fun for the first time.

On her first Mashujaa Day, Mwikali was an easy win for the prize of most accurate representation of a historical figure. Unlike anyone else, she had actually seen her famous ancestor, Syokimau, with her own eyes in a vision and so was able to recreate her ancestor's attire down to the last detail. With bright copper jewellery, a brown leather dress and a small gourd dangling from her waist, she looked every bit the part of Seer and medicine woman.

After studying as many historical images as he could, Odwar looked pretty good too. He was dressed as the invincible warrior Lwanda Magere whose skin it was claimed was as hard as rock and impenetrable by either spear or arrow. He had come to school shirtless with a leopard print tunic around his waist and a spear and shield carried in each hand. Bright white war-paint was smeared all over his body — thankfully covering up the claw marks on his arms — while a chunky animal tooth necklace was fastened around his neck.

Xirsi was dressed as Gasara Winn, legendary hunter of the Aweer people, famous for his ability to commune with animals. He wore nothing but loose, white linen shorts that dropped past his knees and a colourful necklace with large beads that bounced off his chest. A bow and quiver full of arrows hung from one shoulder, while a strikingly beautiful stuffed bird was glued to the other.

Soni, decked out in a rice-white leather skirt with a

matching vest, proudly clenched a long dancing stick in her hand — the unmistakable signature weapon of her ancestor, Cierume, the "dancing warrior". Just like the woman from whom she inherited her powers, Soni was a celebrated dancer. While Cierume used hypnotising dance skills to confuse her opponents in battle, Soni used hers to mesmerise audiences during her performances.

The four impeccably dressed Intasimi Warriors danced and cheered at the Mashujaa Day festival. Traditional drums, and stringed and wind instruments, accompanied a thrilling array of dances put on by students from different ethnic groups. Soni and her troupe were an overwhelming crowd favourite, evidenced by the number of congratulatory high-fives received on the walk back to the school building after the festival was over.

The last dancers had just filed off the stage set up on the sports field when Mwikali broke out into a little dance of her own. "I scored a B on my Swahili exam!" she exclaimed.

"Good job!" Soni whooped. "I didn't even know the exam results were out!"

"They're not... I kind of nagged Bi Macharia into marking my exam before anyone else's," Mwikali confessed, smiling sheepishly. "I couldn't help it — the suspense was killing me!"

"It's a good thing Mrs Amdany isn't around anymore. She would never have agreed to that," Xirsi remarked before dropping his voice down to a hushed whisper. "You know, with her being an actual *monster* and everything."

Odwar shuddered at the memory of how their former teacher, Mrs Amdany, had turned out to be a type of monster called a shiqq. It was during Mwikali's first week at Savanna Academy when she, being the only one able to see their teacher's true bird-faced form, revealed to her new friends what she saw. Thankfully, Mrs Amdany vanished shortly after her evil overlord had been defeated by the Intasimi Warriors and was never to be seen again.

"Speaking of monsters and Intasimi stuff, what's this about us going to Kisumu tomorrow?" Soni asked, turning to Odwar. "*My* folks said that *your* folks said that it was urgent and that we all need to be at your house tomorrow, ready to leave by seven in the morning. *Seven! In the morning!*" She tossed up her hands for emphasis.

Mwikali and Xirsi both murmured reports of similar instructions from their parents, and when they all paused, looking to him for an answer, Odwar knew that the moment had finally come to tell his friends everything.

The field was completely cleared out of all students, leaving the four of them alone in the wide-open space. It was time to come clean about why they were suddenly going to Kisumu, why he had been avoiding them all week, why his life depended on finding his Entasim.

He had so much to say and yet, the words simply curdled in his throat. He glanced down at his feet, willing himself to talk but gagging on his jumbled thoughts instead. His mouth hung open soundlessly, and he ended up looking like a mime, frozen in place.

When something swayed at his feet, Odwar felt a familiar rush of calmness. He waited with an almost-smile for the usual lengthening and widening of his magical shadow, waited for it to rise and wrap itself comfortingly around him, but that never happened. Something else did instead. Something that was straight out of a nightmare. *His* nightmare.

The arms on the shadow below him started to thin and stretch, growing longer and longer until they each seemed several metres long. At their ends, sharp claws began to sprout. Claws that looked like pointed daggers. As if things couldn't get any worse, the daggers suddenly shot up from the ground and reached out to grab him. He swerved in the nick of time, just managing to dodge their razor-sharp ends.

He looked up at his friends to see three baffled faces staring back at him. They couldn't see what he was seeing. They had no idea what was happening. They couldn't help him. So Odwar did the first thing that came into his mind. He turned around and ran. He ran as fast as he could. Away from his friends. Away from his shadow.

Away from his nightmare.

ODWAR VS. THE SHADOW QUEEN

Nail vs. Claw

Mwikali was the first to arrive at Odwar's house on the morning of their trip. Her afro jiggled as she hopped out of her mum's car and skipped towards the veranda where Odwar stood waiting. Her tufts of jet black and cherry red hair matched the baggy "Nairobi" T-shirt she wore over a pair of black biker shorts. Across her chest, a faux leather belt bag hung loosely.

Odwar's nerves twinged when he spotted the bag, knowing that it held Mwikali's Entasim — her divining horn. She had found the clue to its location during a vision of the past. But unlike Mwikali, Odwar wasn't a Seer. *He* didn't have visions. *He* was nowhere near as lucky and was probably going to pay for it in defeat or disaster. Or both.

"Hi!" Mwikali sang, wrapping her arms around him.

Odwar's shadow whipped about playfully as they embraced. Even though it had returned to normal after the bizarre episode in the field the day before, he kept a watchful eye on it and would continue to do so until he found his Entasim.

"Hi, Shadow Odwar," Mwikali said with a giggle as the black cloud began to twist and twirl in front of her face. The shadow was always putting on a show for Mwikali as the newest member of their group, and the one most easily impressed.

"Wait, am I the first to get here?" she asked once it had finally floated down to the ground beneath its owner.

"Yup. A whole twenty minutes early. The driver isn't even here yet." Odwar gestured towards one of the brown wicker chairs arranged around an outdoor table on the porch. "We can chill here as we wait for the others," he suggested, sitting down.

Odwar preferred that they remain outside because inside, his family was seated at the breakfast table. He didn't want his friends to let it slip that the true location of his Entasim was still a mystery. He needed to keep his friends away from Dad and Dad away from the truth.

Mwikali dropped her overnight bag next to Odwar's, by the stairs leading down to the drive, before flopping down into a chair beside him. She lifted and crossed her legs, bringing her chin to rest on her palms, elbows on knees. "I can't believe we're going to Kisumu today. And yesterday, you took off before telling us why! What was up with that by the way?"

Odwar hesitated for a split second then shrugged.

NAIL VS. CLAW

"The car was already in the car park," he lied. "And you know how my dad is. I didn't want him to get mad."

Mwikali's eyes narrowed then dropped to his hands. Odwar suddenly realised that he was rubbing his forearms over the sleeves of his jacket. Now risen from the floor, his shadow was jerking around in the air agitatedly. Odwar bolted upright, fearing the worst: that it would morph into something awful like it had the day before.

"Is everything okay?" Mwikali asked, brows knitted in concern.

He quickly stuffed his hands into the pockets of his joggers. "Yeah, I'm good," he faked.

His shadow stirred one last time before returning to the floor. Mwikali slowly moved her hand to her bag. She patted it gently, eying him curiously.

Odwar should have known better than to lie to a Seer. She could always *see* when something was off. And now, with the divining horn, her intuition was unmatched. He could almost hear the magical objects inside her horn rattling, ratting him out for lying.

He sighed. "Okay, something *is* wrong. But let's wait for the others. I'll tell you all at once."

They didn't have to wait long. Within ten minutes, both Soni and Xirsi had arrived.

ODWAR VS. THE SHADOW QUEEN

Soni popped a straw into her milk box as soon as they had all settled into a half-circle on the outdoor furniture. "So? What's the deal? Why were you so weird yesterday and why're we going to Kit-Mikayi today instead of spending our half term in our beds, sleeping in like normal kids?"

"Oh, I see. Is *that* why you're dressed in pyjamas?" Xirsi teased.

Soni shoved her hand forward, sending a minor sonic tremor in his direction. It knocked the book he was holding — "A Tourist's Guide To Kisumu" — right out of his hand.

"Hey!" Xirsi protested, pouting. "Friends don't use their superpowers on friends!"

Soni had gained a near-perfect handle over her magical abilities. Only a few months before, she had needed total silence and concentration to work her power of manipulating sound. Now, she could send out sonic waves through her hands whilst absent-mindedly sipping on banana-flavoured milk.

The twin buns in her hair tilted as she cocked her head to the side. "What's the point of having superpowers if you can't use them on people who mess with you? Besides, it serves you right for hating on my *travelling* outfit," she stressed. "And this is way better than that touristy khaki fit you have on. Literally *nobody* needs to see those knobbly knees."

Xirsi made an o-shape with his mouth and clutched his heart as if offended. The playful glint in his eyes, however, showed that he was anything but. "For your information, *this* is a travelling outfit." He picked his book off the floor and turned to Odwar. "Speaking of which, why *are* we travelling so soon? I thought the plan was to wait until we had more proof that your Entasim was actually at Kit-Mikayi before we went looking for it. What's changed?"

With all eyes on him, Odwar once again lost the ability to speak. This was becoming frustrating. He was supposed to be the fearless one. The one who led the group, even when situations seemed dangerous. The one with the invincible ancestor. What would they think of him if they knew he was super scared? Of a *dream*?

But that was just the thing. It wasn't just a dream, it was something worse. And that's why he had to come clean. He had to tell them the truth.

"For the past few weeks," he started, his voice quavering, "I've been having this really scary nightmare. It's been getting worse and worse every night, until finally..." He pulled up his sleeves. "This happened."

Mwikali's jaw dropped, her eyes wide as saucers.

Soni rushed towards him. "OHMYGOSH! Are those... scratches? Did you scratch yourself?"

Xirsi popped up on his other side and lifted Odwar's hands to eye level. "These are claw marks, not scratch marks. And d'you see the direction they're going in? Deeper and wider at the elbows and narrow as you get down to the wrists. He couldn't have done this to himself. Someone — some*thing* — did this to him."

Unsurprisingly, Xirsi was quick to work out that it was claws and not fingernails that had bruised Odwar's skin. He was, after all, the animal expert.

"Something attacked you while you were asleep?" Mwikali asked, her voice muffled by the palm held over it.

"That's just the thing. I sleep with my door and windows locked. Nobody else was in my room." Odwar yanked back his hands from Xirsi's investigative gaze. "This happened while I was asleep. It happened in my dream."

Soni's face scrunched up. "Hold up. You think something scratched — sorry, *clawed* you — in your dream? And you woke up with the marks in real life?"

He nodded slowly, knowing how crazy it sounded. "I don't think it was just a nightmare. I think it was somehow...*real*."

NAIL VS. CLAW

"Bro...that sounds..." Xirsi frowned, bunching up his curly hair between his fingers.

"Crazy? I know!" Odwar said, completing his friend's thought. "But I'm telling you guys. This nightmare, it's nothing like anything I've ever had. I'm somewhere cold and mouldy and dark. So dark that I can hardly see anything. And my shadow isn't there. I'm all alone except for these...creatures. I can feel them all around me. White glowing eyes in the dark. But there's something else. Something worse out there. I can't quite see it and it only moves when I close my eyes. When I blink. It's coming towards me, coming to get me. It gets closer and closer each night. The other night, it got close enough to grab hold of me. I screamed, and when I woke up," he looked down at his forearms, "I had these."

They stared at him in round-eyed astonishment.

"I believe you," Mwikali suddenly declared. She jutted out a pointy finger at Soni and Xirsi. "And you guys should believe him too. We said we'd always believe each other, remember? Have each other's backs?"

When the other two nodded slowly in agreement, she turned back confidently to Odwar. "We believe you. But, Odwar, if you've been having nightmares for so long, why're you only telling us now?"

Because I was embarrassed and didn't want you guys to

think I was weak.

"Because I needed to come up with a plan first," he said. "If I can find my Entasim, I just know that the nightmares will stop. Or even if they don't, having it will give me the strength I need to face whatever it is that's trying to get me. And I have to find it quickly, or who knows what will happen the next time. Until then? Don't let me fall asleep!"

Just then, a white seven-seater van beeped as it crept up the drive towards the house. The four friends stood up, and once they had loaded their bags and climbed inside, Soni and Mwikali, who were seated in the front, twisted around to face Odwar.

"When did the nightmares start?"

"Do you have them every single night?"

"Almost every night," Odwar revealed, staring out of the window as they began their eight-hour journey. "And it all started after we went around Kit-Mikayi — the *fake* Kit-Mikayi — a few weeks ago. You know how we all felt different afterwards?"

The three friends smiled back at him knowingly, remembering how they had stumbled upon a pile of rocks in their school chapel that had changed them forever. The four had circled round the rocks and, rather than dying like the myths had said they would, they had ended up stronger than ever before.

That stone tower at their school, which resembled a very real one in Kisumu known as Kit-Mikayi, granted them enhanced abilities. Mwikali could now predict movements during combat, making her an excellent fighter; Soni no longer needed silence for her sonic blasts; and Xirsi could communicate with all animals, not just birds.

As for Odwar, his shadow had lifted off the ground for the very first time, turning itself into a gust of black smoke. It was no longer bound to the ground as before, but free to move around and blind any monster unlucky enough to get caught up in it. But that's not all that changed. When he had gone to bed that night, he had discovered that the rocks had done something else to him too.

"I had my first nightmare that very night — creatures in the dark, with one more sinister than the rest, coming towards me. That night I... I..."

He clenched his jaw and dug his fingernails into his palms. He was *not* about to tell his friends that he had wet the bed the first time he had had the nightmare.

"That night I was terrified," he continued, choosing to leave out the most embarrassing bit. "And I've been having the same nightmare ever since."

"But if they're getting worse," Xirsi said, glancing worriedly at Odwar's arms, "shouldn't we tell Mr Lemayian about them?"

Odwar shook his head furiously. "No! He'll only try and stop us from going after my Entasim. He'll say it's too dangerous, especially now that monsters in the underworld know that we're the Intasimi Warriors. He'll tell us to keep a low profile and wait."

"Well maybe we *should* wait," Mwikali countered. "Besides, Mr Lemayian has been around for a long, loooong time. Maybe he knows who or what this thing in your dreams is."

Odwar thought about it for a moment. Mwikali did have a point. Their mentor, Mr Lemayian, wasn't just their headmaster, a historian and an Intasimi bloodlines expert, he was also an immortal Oloibon — a spiritual teacher who had guided warriors for centuries. There was a chance he could help them figure this all out, but there was also a chance he would stop them from going after his Entasim altogether. Odwar couldn't risk it.

"We'll tell him...soon. Let's just get to Kit-Mikayi first and find my Entasim. Then... Then we'll... We'll..." He yawned, suddenly feeling like all energy had been zapped out of him. "We'll tell him everything."

Odwar's head felt like a giant-sized boulder rolling

around on his shoulders and he was having trouble keeping his eyes open. Everything around him grew hazy and everyone around him seemed to be moving in slow motion, like they were all drifting inside a giant bowl of honey. He slouched in his seat. Maybe he could close his eyes for just a few seconds...

Soni gripped his shoulder. "Hey! You said we can't let you fall asleep! C'mon, sit up."

"Okaaay," he replied, sluggishly. "But lemme just rest for two seconds... Just, like, two seconds..."

"Odwar, wake up!" Mwikali cried.

But the world around him was already fading to black.

Xirsi squished Odwar's face with both hands. He was saying something about not giving into the nightmare but his voice sounded like it was coming from lightyears away.

The last thing Odwar saw before the darkness swallowed him up was his shadow whooshing around him.

The last thing he heard was his friends shouting his name.

ODWAR VS. THE SHADOW QUEEN

Shadow Prince vs. Shadow World

The thing hovering in the air was a large, jagged-edged creature cloaked in the deepest hues of blue and purple. Its arms were abnormally long, with sharp claws that dragged along the ground. A pair of white orbs burned from the creature's spiky head directly into Odwar. Those eyes were the first thing he saw when his nightmare began. Fear had turned his legs into trees that remained rooted to the spot. Unable to move, all he could do was stare into the monster's face.

"Welcome to the world of shadows," the thing rasped, lowering slowly towards him. "I've been waiting for you."

There was no opening for a mouth on its face, but even so, it had a voice that thrummed sharply in Odwar's ears. Suddenly, and without warning, the creature reached down and grabbed his arms. Its grip felt strong enough to crush bones to powder, and Odwar cried out as blinding pain rippled through his body.

"I knew it was only a matter of time before I pulled you fully into my world," the creature gloated. Rotten-smelling blasts of air slammed into his face with every word.

Odwar squeezed his eyes shut and scrunched his shoulders. "It's just a nightmare. I'm still in the van. I just need to wake up. *Please* wake up," he whimpered.

"Oh, this isn't just a nightmare. You're in another world. *My* world. And you can't leave unless I want you to."

Sickness rose inside him. Did it say he was trapped in *another world*?

"What... What do you mean?" he choked out. "How? How am I...?"

The creature let go of his arms and shot into the air with a cackle. "How are you in two worlds at the same time?" it cut in excitedly. "Why, your shadow of course! The same substance that makes up your shadow, makes up this world. The two are connected!"

The dark creature whirled around the spot where it stood. "Some time ago, the barrier between our worlds was weakened. And then I started to hear whispers from the beastly ones. They told me about the Intasimi Warriors. About one who could see monsters in true form, another who could use sound to cause damage, and another who could control animals. And finally, about the boy with a magical shadow. They thought I might like to know there was another like me — a shadowy being — in this other world."

In a flash, the monster swooped down, bringing its devilish eyes within inches of Odwar's. His knees turned to jelly as white balls of fire burned into him. It breathed the next words into his face. "You see, my dear shadow prince, I'm the ruler of all shadows. Your Queen. And? Your *mother*."

The darkness seemed to rage like an angry sea around Odwar. Shock, confusion and disbelief threatened to drown him. He rocked back on his heels, dizzied by what he had just heard.

"*Mother?*" he mouthed.

But he already had a mother. His mother was a gentle but firm, busy but loving woman. His mother took him on Mummy Mondays. His mother was human and in his world. She was not this *thing*.

The creature scoffed. "Mother, grandmother, great great great grandmother...it's all the same to me. My husband was none other than Lwanda Magere, your ancestor, which makes *me* your grandmother. Several times removed, of course."

"You're Lwanda Magere's wife?" Odwar balked at the thought. How could she still be alive? Why was she a monster?

From all the stories he had heard, Lwanda Magere's

wife, Mikayi, was a sweet lady. This didn't make any sense! Then he remembered how back in the old days, men would marry several wives at a time. So, maybe this wasn't his *first* wife... Maybe this was...

Dread washed over him as the answer came. This wasn't Mikayi. This was the other wife, the wife nobody dared speak of. The one who led Lwanda Magere to his death. The one who betrayed him.

"His *second* wife," she confirmed.

The legend of Lwanda Magere and his wives, told to him since he was a toddler, came flooding back into his memory all at once. Of how he was the fiercest warrior Western Kenya had ever known. How he could knock out a thousand men with one blow. How the sharpest weapons bounced off his rock-hard skin without leaving a mark. How he was invincible. And how it all ended when his second wife revealed to his enemies the secret to his strength: his shadow. Her betrayal led to his death and to her being forever remembered as the woman who had killed the greatest warrior of all time.

Odwar stared up at the saw-edged, billowy shape hovering above him. A writhing cloud of murky dark vapours. This thing was once...*human?*

"The War Council found out what I'd done to their beloved warrior," she continued, with acid-like bitterness lacing her words. "And so they summoned a jajuok, an evil wizard, who used his powers to banish my soul to this realm."

Something cried out in the darkness. Another thing moaned. The very air around them seemed to groan in misery.

"I was furious, confused and bitter when I awoke. Every emotion I felt turned my body into a shadow of itself, and birthed one of them." She pointed a long, ragged claw into the surrounding wilderness. "I call them shadow spawn. They are the offspring of my rage, and I am their queen. *Your* queen..."

He shook his head hard and fast. "I'm not one of your... You're not my..."

"*You* are as much a part of this world as I am, little shadow prince," she snarled. "You belong here. With me."

Without warning, she jerked forwards and choked Odwar. Her touch was freezing cold and burned like an ice cube held against the skin for too long. He tried to cry out but could only sob as frost bit its way up his neck. Crackling sounds reached his ears as his body stiffened under her grip.

"We belong together," she wheezed, leaning into him so that her large, white eyes were all he could see.

The numbing chill had now spread throughout his body. Blood drummed in his ears. Shadowy figures danced in and out of focus. The suffocating smell of rot filled his nose. Tears slipped down his face as he felt himself turning into a corpse.

This is it, he thought, sorrowfully. *I'm never going to see my friends or family again.*

His eyes closed with one final thought.

It's all over.

The Team vs. Kit-Mikayi

He blinked.

More darkness.

Blinked again.

Still dark, but...

Odwar breathed a ragged sigh of relief. He recognised the black smoke that surrounded him now. It was his shadow. He was awake.

"Odwar!"

Mwikali's panicked scream startled him, and as his shadow drifted down to the floor of the van, the horrified faces of his friends came into view.

"You've been asleep for *hours*," Mwikali shrieked. "We've been trying to wake you up, but nothing was working!"

"I'm okay," Odwar croaked. His throat felt like it was lined with sandpaper.

Xirsi's usually golden-brown face was ashen. Odwar had never seen his friend look so scared. "We couldn't see through your shadow. Didn't know if you were asleep or...worse."

Soni, who always had something to say, was both tongue-tied and goggle-eyed as she stared back at him.

"Wait, how long have I been asleep?" He looked outside the windows at the rolling green hills on either side of the road and instantly knew the answer. They were already in Kisumu. He had been asleep the entire journey. The whole eight hours.

"What was going on?" Xirsi asked. "You were yelling and screaming... Was it another nightmare?"

Odwar leaned forward, shaking his head. "It wasn't just a nightmare. It was worse. I was in another *world*." He went on to tell them everything. About the world of shadows, the shadow spawn and the monstrous queen that ruled over them. He didn't leave out a single detail, even pausing to break down the history of Lwanda Magere and his second wife's betrayal.

In turn, Xirsi showed him a video he'd recorded during the nightmare. It showed Odwar's shadow completely blanketing his body in a thick, impenetrable cloud. From somewhere inside the black mass, Odwar heard the spine chilling sounds of his own screams.

Leaning away from Xirsi's phone with a shudder, he used both hands to peel back the collar of his jacket. "She also did this."

Soni's hand flew to her mouth while Xirsi and

THE TEAM VS. KIT-MIKAYI

Mwikali gasped and drew back in horror.

Odwar pulled his phone from his pocket, clicked the reverse camera on it and brought the device up to his neck. Claw-shaped bruises marked his flesh. The welts were right where he knew they would be, right where the monster had strangled him.

"She wanted to trap me there...in the shadow world," he explained to his friends. "And if I don't find my Entasim, if she pulls me back in there one more time—"

"Well, that's not gonna happen," Soni said, finally finding her voice. "Because we're going to find your Entasim and you're going to be strong enough to stand up to this shadowy monster woman."

"Shadowy monster woman?" Mwikali asked with a quizzical look on her face.

Soni shrugged. "You know what I mean! The monster in charge of the shadow world, the—"

"Shadow Queen!" Xirsi exclaimed, snapping his fingers. "That's what we're gonna call her: the Shadow Queen."

Soni snorted out a laugh. "*Wow*. The Shadow Queen? A little dramatic don't you think?"

"She's shrouded in dark vapours, has claws, glowing eyes *and* reproduces spawn babies when she's feeling down. She's already dramatic," Xirsi argued.

At that moment, the driver lowered the partition screen that separated him from the rear seats and turned down the volume on the car radio. "Odwar, we're going to Kit-Mikayi first, yah?"

"No," Odwar answered quickly. "We'll drop these guys at the house first. I'm going there by myself."

He had made the decision to leave his friends out of his plans as soon as he woke up. This latest nightmare had shown him that whatever was going on with him was more serious than he had imagined. The last thing he wanted to do was put them in any unnecessary danger.

"I'm going to Kit-Mikayi alone," he repeated, ignoring the hurt looks on their faces. "This could be really dangerous. And it's my thing, my problem to deal with."

"Are you serious?" Soni huffed. "There's no such thing as *your* problem. We're a team. It's our problem. We do this together."

Xirsi's brown curls bounced as he nodded. "Bro, this isn't just 'your thing' anymore. We're all a part of it now."

"Don't you remember what Mr Lemayian said?" Mwikali chipped in. "Our bond — our Intasimi Warrior bond — strengthens our *individual* powers. We're stronger when we stick together."

Odwar bit his lower lip as he stared out of the window. A slew of questions streamed through his mind: Were his friends right about sticking together? Was it wrong to drag them into his mess? Would he even find his Entasim?

Before he could come up with any answers, Soni had leaned forward and tapped the partition screen. "We're *all* going to Kit-Mikayi," she said to the driver once it was lowered. Turning back to Odwar, she fixed him with a not-up-for-debate glare. "We're sticking together."

The driver made a sharp U-turn and grunted as he pressed down on the accelerator.

"Guys, what if something terrible happens when we go around the rocks this time?" Odwar asked, accepting that his friends were coming with him whether he liked it or not. "What if the veil between our world and the shadow world grows even weaker? What if we black out when we go around Kit-Mikayi, but this time, we never wake up?"

Mwikali flipped open the sketchbook that had been sitting on her lap and held it open for him to see. "I don't think that's gonna happen. I think we're going to be okay."

The drawing on the page showed the four of them standing at the foot of the Kit-Mikayi rocks, holding hands and smiling. The sight brought on a surge of hope in Odwar. They had all learned to trust Mwikali's drawings of the future. It was how her powers as a Seer had first manifested — everything she drew in her sketchbook came true.

"I drew this about two hours into the trip. It came to me when we were all trying to figure out what was wrong with you," she told him. "You see how happy we all are? All together? I know nothing bad will happen to us, just like I know that we need to do this with you."

Odwar's eyes welled up as a mixture of pride and fear for his friends filled his heart. "Okay. We do this together, as a team," he agreed.

"Exactly," Mwikali said with a smile. "And before you ask the same question these guys already did: no, I can't use my powers to see where your Entasim is. I've already tried. And I have a feeling it's going to be the same for all the Entasims. Come to think of it, it was the same for mine too. I may have got a clue from a vision about where to go, but in the end, I had to find it on my own."

Within minutes, the van slowed down and eventually came to a stop. Through the windshield, a rock formation the height of an Egyptian pyramid towered in the distance. The giant grey boulders that made up Kit-Mikayi were stacked high atop each other in separate piles, giving the prehistoric monument an air of mystery and might.

With a pounding heart, Odwar stepped out of the car

and led his friends towards what he hoped would be the solution to all his problems — his Entasim.

*

"Stone of the first wife. That's what Kit-Mikayi means in the Luo language," the tour guide belted out from the foot of the monument. "And that's because when the first settlers stumbled upon this site, one of them fell in love with these rocks. He began to spend so much time here that people started to refer to the stones as his first wife. Kit means 'stone of' and Mikayi, 'first wife'. Kit-Mikayi."

Xirsi sighed impatiently, eyeing the ten or so tourists hanging onto the guide's every word. "We can't do what we need to do with all these people milling around," he grumbled.

"It's fine. The guide goes on break in about…" Odwar glanced at his phone screen, "five minutes. We'll do it when he leaves."

Having visited Kit-Mikayi with his family dozens of times, Odwar knew everything there was to know about it, including the fact that this particular tour guide, a lanky silver-haired man with several missing teeth, never skipped his 4pm tea break.

"Are we ready?" Soni asked when the coast was clear.

"Let's get this over with. It's hotter than two goats farting in a wool blanket."

The day was definitely sweltering and the characteristically hot sun of Western Kenya burned bright against a cloudless sky. They took time to wipe sweat from their foreheads before linking damp hands together.

"It serves you right for wearing those thick pyjamas," Xirsi teased, prompting giggles from the other two.

In that moment, with hands joined and smiles on their faces, Odwar realised that they looked exactly like they did in Mwikali's drawing. He also realised that most of his fears had melted away into excitement. This would work! He was going to find his Entasim. He had to. "Let's do this," he said excitedly, tugging them forward.

According to legend, they had to go around Kit-Mikayi seven times. Upon the last turn, they would either die or be reborn anew. Soni pointed out that being turned into goats was also an option but there was no proof of it ever having happened. The last time they went round magical rocks, they were "reborn" with newly-improved powers.

Odwar eagerly dragged them around the tower at jogging pace for the first four rotations. It wasn't easy. The rocks were perched on an incline, rising up through dense bush. He felt bad for not warning his friends that going around Kit-Mikayi was going to be quite a hike. They huffed and puffed their way around the natural monument, whacking thorny branches out of their way as they did so.

It was upon the fifth turn that it dawned on Odwar that he felt...normal. Not eerily tired like he had the last time they went around the tower of rocks. He began to fear that this wasn't going to go according to plan.

"I don't think this is working," Mwikali said as they finished their sixth turn.

"Yeah, I feel nothing," Soni agreed.

"Let's just keep going," Odwar urged, sounding a little desperate. "Maybe... Maybe this time will be different."

Halfway through their last spin around Kit-Mikayi, the sky suddenly grew dark. What was once clear blue became a sea of black clouds. Odwar could feel his muscles tense up and his stomach twist as they neared the finishing point. Memories of the Shadow Queen flashed in his mind — her glowing eyes, long claws around his neck, the feeling of his body turning to ice. This had to work, or else—

BOOM!

A loud rumble rocked the air, shaking the ground beneath them.

CRACK!

The sky flashed as bright light streaked across the heavens above.

Odwar flung himself onto the ground and closed his eyes, bracing himself for what he knew was coming: a few minutes of unconsciousness, followed by an awakening to find the stones of Kit-Mikayi pulled apart and his Entasim buried within.

Several seconds of agonizing silence crept by before something wet landed on his cheek, followed by another, then another. He opened his eyes and scrambled to his feet as the initial droplets of rain turned into a full-on shower.

"It's just a storm," Xirsi yelled above the sound of pounding rain. "It didn't work."

They had come to a stop where they had started, having gone around the rocks all seven times. Nothing had happened. No black out, no magical transformation, no Entasim. Just bucketfuls of rain.

Soni turned towards the car. "Let's get out of here!"

"Guys, please, we have to try again," Odwar pleaded as thunderclaps beat around them. "I have nowhere else to look. If I don't find my Entasim here...that's it. It's all over for me."

They moaned and groaned, but in the end, they did as

he asked. Through the pelting rain, they began to circle Kit-Mikayi once more.

Odwar clenched his fists as they walked, praying with every step that the rocks would magically tumble apart and reveal his ancestral heirloom, praying that this desperate plan to find it would work.

But it didn't.

They completed the seventh turn and still, nothing.

Soni put an encouraging arm around Odwar's shoulder. "Don't worry, we'll keep looking. We won't stop trying until we find it."

"And we can ask Mr Lemayian for help with your nightmares and the Shadow Queen. We'll figure everything out when we get back home," Xirsi added.

Odwar stared into the distance dazedly and followed his friends back into the van. Fear and disappointment churned in his chest making it hard to think. How would he defeat the Shadow Queen now? And at some point, he would have to sleep. What would happen to him then?

A buzz in his pocket yanked him away from his thoughts. It was a text message from his father: *Waiting for you at the house. Looking forward to seeing your Entasim.*

Odwar threw his head back and sunk low into the seat. Just when he thought things couldn't get any worse, they just had.

ODWAR VS. THE SHADOW QUEEN

Real Orengo vs. Fake Orengo

Odwar's family home was a hive of activity. Catering staff in stiff khaki uniforms buzzed around the brilliant white tent that extended across the front yard. Platters of freshly roasted goat meat and steaming hot pilau were being generously served to tables of guests.

"Your uncle is lucky the rain has stopped," the van driver remarked as he helped to unload the car. "All of this is for his harambee, the fundraiser for his campaign. He needs it to go well, you know? He's running for governor."

Odwar distractedly nodded in response as he took note of several burly bodyguards lining the edges of their compound. His uncle never went anywhere without them, and they were known to be rough and vicious, just like their boss.

Xirsi whistled and shook his head as they carried their bags up a long flight of stairs leading to the gleaming three-storey mansion. "Your Kisumu house is even larger than your Nairobi house!"

Odwar hardly heard a word. All he could think about

was his Entasim and how angry his father would be that he didn't have it. What would he do when he learned that Odwar had lied about knowing where it was?

As they walked through the house's large Moroccan-style doors, his friends oohed and aahed at the grand foyer and majestic staircase that appeared before them. They giggled excitedly when a team of house staff swooped in to show them to the guest bedrooms on the first floor.

Odwar was blind to everything and everyone as he trudged up the extra flight of stairs to the floor he shared with Gor. Throwing his bedroom door open, he belly-flopped onto his bed and buried his face in his pillow.

"Is everything okay?"

He nearly jumped out of his skin. Making sure to quickly rub his tear-stained face against his forearms, Odwar flipped around to find his grandmother standing at the doorway.

As usual, she wore a boldly-patterned headwrap and a matching dress that flowed down to her ankles. While his grandmother's body might have been hunched over and frail, her greyish eyes were sharper than ever, and they studied him closely as she moved towards him.

"I'm fine, Dana. I'm okay," he said as he stood and reached down to give her a hug. "Just tired."

She was quiet for a moment before inviting him to sit down on the bed beside her. "How long have I known you?" she asked, head cocked.

Odwar knew where this was going and sighed. "Since before I was born," he answered in a sing-song voice.

"Since before you were born," she repeated immediately after him. "I knew your mother was pregnant even before she did. And I knew how special you would be."

Odwar dropped his chin to his chest. Would she still think he was special knowing how afraid he was, or how he had failed to find his Entasim?

"Are you having problems with your father again?" she probed knowingly.

He bit his bottom lip and fought back the tears threatening to spill from his eyes.

His grandmother pulled him close and rocked side to side comfortingly. "My husband — your grandfather — was the same as your father. A hard, hard man. Impossible to please. Your father tried everything to make that man proud. Everything. But all my husband ever cared about was one of his sons becoming the Intasimi descendant."

Odwar's ears perked up. He had never heard this story before. His grandfather had died decades before he was born and Dad never talked about him.

"When your father reached the age of fourteen, your grandfather knew that it wouldn't be him. He wouldn't inherit the gift. So he became convinced that it had to be our youngest son — your uncle— who would get it. From that moment on, it was as if your father didn't exist. All my husband cared about was your uncle."

Odwar's eyes widened as everything suddenly made sense. No wonder Dad had always favoured his elder brother, Gor, over him. It was because Dad's own father had always done the opposite — favoured his younger brother over *him*, the first born. Dad was making up for the fact that he had grown up as the unfairly-treated older brother by doing the reverse with his sons!

"I loved my husband, but his obsession with the Intasimi power cost him a relationship with his first-born son. With your dad. A relationship they never got to mend. He died when they were still teenagers. And maybe it's just as well. The disappointment of neither one of his sons inheriting the gift might have been too much for him to bear."

She squeezed Odwar's shoulder before pulling back. "Instead, it was your father who got to see one of his sons become the Intasimi descendant."

"Dad wishes it was Gor who got the gift," Odwar spat

REAL ORENGO VS. FAKE ORENGO

out. "Gor is braver, bigger...stronger than I am. It should have been him."

His grandmother's wrinkled face brightened with a chuckle. "True strength is in the heart and spirit, not muscles! True strength comes from *inside*."

Before Odar had a chance to respond, sounds of singing and cheering floated into the room and drew them both to the window. There, they saw a convoy of black SUVs streaming through the gate. Throngs of traditional dancers were lined up on either side of the drive, welcoming Odwar's uncle with drum and song.

Out of the back window of one of the cars, Uncle Cyrus leaned over to greet the crowd with a toothy grin and a wave of his signature fly whisk.

"That should have been your father's," Grandmother said quietly. "That orengo he swings around so proudly shouldn't be his. It should have been left to the eldest son."

For as long as Odwar could remember, Uncle Cyrus had carried around an orengo — a fly whisk with a brown wooden handle, fitted with the bushy black hairs of a bull's tail. The orengo was a symbol of power, only given to a select few in the Luo community, and Uncle Cyrus never went anywhere without it. Some people even said that it had magical powers...

"Where did that orengo come from?" Odwar asked, feeling the hairs on the back of his neck stand up.

Grandmother squinted her eyes, deep in thought. "Well, let's see. Your grandfather got it from his father who got it from his. It's been in our family for decades, maybe even longer. And when your grandfather died, instead of it being inherited by your father — the eldest son — Cyrus took it for himself."

Odwar's hammering heart sent him shooting up from the bed. He shuffled excitedly from foot to foot as he spoke. "Could it... Could it have belonged to Lwanda Magere? Is it that old?"

"It's possible. I don't see why not. Why? Do you think it might be—" she started, but Odwar was already sprinting out of the room.

*

"You want us to steal your Uncle Cyrus' fly whisk?" Soni exclaimed. "The one he never lets out of his sight?"

"I want us to *swap* it. With this." Odwar held out the fly whisk he had just dug out of storage. It had been a gift to his father from a political rival that had remained stuffed at the back of a closet for years. "You see the handle? It's exactly the same as Uncle Cyrus'.

REAL ORENGO VS. FAKE ORENGO

The only problem is that the hairs on this one are totally different."

Xirsi ran his fingers through the black hairs. "Yeah, this one's made from horse hair. Your uncle's fly whisk is made of bull hair. Different texture, different colours..." He shook his head. "There's no way a swap will work."

"I know. That's why the first thing we need to do is rip off the hairs on this one and replace them with a bull's," Odwar said, pushing the fly whisk into Xirsi's chest. "And you're the only person I know who can get me close enough to a bull to pull that off."

"Hold up! Where on earth are we even going to find a bull?" Soni demanded.

Odwar was already speed-walking towards the front door. "Follow me!"

A few minutes later they were standing in front of a bull pen, one of the many animal enclosures that sat at the back of the Kisumu mansion. The pen stood apart from all the others and was secured by three half-height concrete walls and a reinforced metal gate.

"Are we sure about this?" Mwikali whispered, eyeing the snorting bull. Having been nearly kicked over by a cow before, she was less eager than the others to keep going with the mission.

"It'll be okay. He's just a little anxious, that's all,"

Xirsi said reassuringly. He started to glide his hands through the air like he did every time he communed with animals. And as he waved his hands, the bull's upturned ears relaxed while its violently flicking tail flopped into a relaxed position.

"Mwikali, Soni, start feeding it," Xirsi ordered, pointing at a bale of hay. "Odwar, start cutting the hair. We need to move quickly. I'm not sure how long I can keep him calm."

While the girls palmed handfuls of hay into the hypnotised animal's mouth, Odwar crept around to its tail with a pair of scissors. He was relieved to see that the tone and texture of the bull's hairs matched those on his uncle's fly whisk perfectly.

Once positioned, he crouched and leaned forward, but just as his trembling fingers grazed the bull's black tail, it jolted violently and spun its enormous body around to face him. With bowed head and enlarged nostrils, it began to paw at the ground.

"*Nobody. Move,*" Xirsi gritted out.

Odwar stumbled back, ready to wheel around and run, but Xirsi's glare stopped him in his tracks.

"Never turn your back on a bull. It *will* chase you. And it *will* get you," he warned.

Odwar's eyes were deadlocked with the animal's,

his mouth hanging open in a silent scream. The bull's massive shoulders hunched as it shook its two giant horns. "What...do...I...do?" he panted.

Xirsi didn't answer. He simply closed his eyes and lifted his hands higher into the air, waving them around like a martial arts grandmaster. Slowly, the bull turned its head towards him, and like a puppet on a string, went back to its original standing position.

This time, Odwar didn't hesitate. As soon as the bull settled in front of him once more, he picked up its tail with one finger and snipped away. Working as quickly as possible, he was able to gather a fluffy bundle of long black strands of hair.

With their prize secured, the four friends cautiously reversed out of the pen and then returned to the house. There, they carefully glued the new hairs onto the fake fly whisk.

Odwar was proud of the result. It didn't look exactly like the one Uncle Cyrus had, but it was close enough to pass a non-thorough inspection. Feeling confident, he stuffed the fly whisk into his pocket and led his friends outside.

"Now comes the hard part," he warned. He and the others were seated around a plastic table, one of the many dotted inside the large outdoor tent. His eyes were glued to the high table at the front where Uncle Cyrus and other VIPs, including his father, sat on a podium. Odwar avoided his father's piercing gaze as he studied the group, knowing that Dad would beckon him over and demand to see his Entasim the minute they made eye contact.

Not much longer, he thought. If this plan worked, he would have something to show Dad. *But if not...* No, he wouldn't let his mind go there. This had to work.

He turned his focus to the centre of the high table where the fly whisk lay next to his uncle's large heaping of food. "We need to make the swap without Uncle, his bodyguards or anyone else noticing."

"And how on earth are we gonna do that?" Mwikali wondered.

Xirsi smiled cheekily. He tilted his head to the side and touched his fingers together like an evil-genius. "I think I have an idea..." he said.

Dad vs. the Bull

Odwar approached his uncle holding a mouth-watering platter of goat ribs. And, just as expected, Uncle Cyrus' eyes lit up with greedy delight the instant they laid sight on the bounty of meat. The long, rectangular high table at which he and the other VIPs sat was mounted on a stage and stood facing the rest of the guests at their round tables. Uncle Cyrus could barely contain himself as Odwar inched towards his seat at the centre of the table. He rocked back and forth eagerly, blinking frequently and smacking his lips together.

Out of the corner of his eye, Odwar spotted his friends swinging into action. Xirsi's fingers danced in the air, directing a thick swarm of flies towards the bodyguards. The oversized men swatted around helplessly and were soon too distracted to notice Uncle Cyrus' fly whisk rolling towards the edge of the table under Soni's control. She repeatedly pumped out her hands, releasing sonic waves strong enough to keep it moving in the right direction.

Nobody paid them any attention. In fact, the only

person who seemed to notice that something odd was happening was Gor who was seated with their grandmother at a table not far from the stage. Gor peered curiously at Odwar for a second, then shrugged and shook his head in that "None of my business" way he did when it came to anything Intasimi-related. He soon went back to chatting with Grandmother and eating his food while lazily scrolling on his phone.

The heist could go on as planned.

"Hi, Uncle Cyrus!" Odwar sang, locking in his uncle's attention so that he wouldn't see what was happening right under his nose. "Would you like some of this nyama choma? Chef says that it's the best roast meat he's ever made."

Uncle Cyrus hummed in anticipation as his fat fingers hovered over the platter. His eyes roamed the dish hungrily, searching around for the largest rib. As he was busy plucking a mammoth-sized chunk from the heap, his fly whisk tipped off the edge of the table and dropped to the ground where Mwikali was crouched, waiting to catch it. Hidden by table drapery and using her motion prediction powers, she had crawled under the table and weaved her way through pairs of legs to get into position. Then, with her amazingly quick reflexes, she snatched the fly whisk out of the air before it hit the floor.

DAD VS. THE BULL

Xirsi's plan was working perfectly. Now, all Mwikali needed to do was—

"*Aye!* You! What are you doing over there?"

Time seemed to stand still as Uncle Cyrus dropped the giant rib he held in his hand and snapped his gaze, first to the big bald man walking towards him, and then to the small girl at his feet at whom the shouting bodyguard was pointing.

In two large strides the guard was at their side, yanking Mwikali off the ground and plopping her down in front of Uncle Cyrus. The guests at the high table bristled at the disturbance for a brief moment before getting back to gnawing on their meat.

"What's going on here?" Uncle growled, meat-coloured spittle flying out of his mouth.

Odwar stepped sideways to shield Mwikali from his rage. "This is my friend, Mwikali," he sputtered. "She was just… She was just…"

"I was just picking this up," Mwikali cut in, slipping out from behind Odwar to place Uncle Cyrus' fly whisk back on the table.

There was a tense moment of silence as Uncle Cyrus eyed the fly whisk and the two of them suspiciously. Then, eager to carry on with his feast, he seized the entire meat platter from Odwar and waved a dismissive hand behind his head. "Go, get them out of here."

With a rough hand around the back of their necks, the two were shepherded out of the tent by the foul-tempered bodyguard.

They thought that that would be the end of it, but as soon as the tent flap closed behind them, the bald man twisted their bodies around to face him. "You little liars are going to tell me exactly what you were doing," he snarled, bringing his face so close that they could count the hairs poking out of his nose.

Odwar knew he should feel scared of him, but all he felt in that moment was overwhelming sadness. Their plan to swap the fly whisk had failed, interrupted by the one bodyguard who had somehow escaped Xirsi's insect attack. With Uncle leaving for another part of the country as soon as his harambee was over, Odwar knew he had lost his best chance to get the Entasim. He had lost his chance to save himself from the Shadow Queen.

"We don't know what you're talking about," he retorted, wriggling out of the man's grasp. He was about to say something worse, maybe about how the guy's breath smelled like rotten eggs, when he noticed that Mwikali had grown deathly still. Her eyes were tightly closed and her breathing shaky. A spike of fear went shooting down Odwar's spine as he looked back and forth between his friend and the bodyguard, realising what was going on.

Mwikali only behaved like this, she was only *this* terrified, when she saw one thing: monsters in true form. When monsters were angry, like this bodyguard was, Seers with special magical sight like Mwikali could see through their disguise of human skin. Right at that moment, she could see this bodyguard's hidden *monster* face.

If Odwar had to guess, he would say that the man was an ogre. Mwikali had once told them that in true form ogres were green with hollow black pits for eyes, bull rings in their bulbous noses and large lower canine teeth that jutted out of wide, drooling mouths. Ogres were also wild, unpredictable and extremely dangerous when they were mad.

"I know you can see my true form Seer-girl. Do you think I care? I'm not scared of you," the bodyguard growled at Mwikali who still had her eyes squeezed shut. "And you, shadow boy — we told the one who rules the world of shadows all about you. It's only a matter of time before she gets you once and for all."

Quick as lightning, he released Odwar and scooped Mwikali up with both hands.

"OPEN YOUR EYES!" he roared.

ODWAR VS. THE SHADOW QUEEN

With a quick glance around to make sure they were alone, Odwar summoned his shadow from the ground. It rushed into the air and enveloped the ogre in a cone-shaped tornado. Blind and terrified, he yelled out in confusion and dropped Mwikali back onto the ground.

While the ogre bodyguard was groping around in the thick black cloud surrounding him, Odwar grabbed Mwikali's hand. "Run!" he shouted.

The two raced to find Soni and Xirsi. Once reunited, Odwar rushed them out of the tent and into the house. They tore up the stairs and had just made it to his bedroom door when someone yanked Odwar's arm and spun him around.

"Odwar."

A worm of sweat slithered down Odwar's neck. "Hi, Dad," he gulped.

At some point during the scuffle with the bodyguard, Odwar's father must have come to the house looking for him and decided to wait, skulking around the corner from his bedroom, remaining just out of sight, like a predator stalking its prey.

"I've been looking for you," his father said sternly. "And I believe you have something to show me?"

Odwar's mind muddied. A thousand different excuses blundered through it, none of them seeming strong enough to save him.

"I... I..." He scratched the back of his head, convinced that Maina's brain farts must be contagious.

Just then, something fuzzy rubbed up against his upheld hand. Something that felt like...hair? From behind him, someone plucked his fingers open and wrapped them around an object that was hard and smooth. A handle? He grabbed hold of the item and then flung his hand forward to see what it was.

It was an orengo. Uncle Cyrus' orengo. The *real* one.

He glanced back to find Mwikali beaming at him. She had done it! At some point during the scuffle at the high table, perhaps when he had stepped in front of her, Mwikali had pulled out the fake fly whisk from his back pocket and swapped it for the real one.

Odwar flashed her a grateful smile before turning to face his father. "I *do* have something to show you. Dad, I present to you my Entasi—"

The change happened in the blink of an eye. So fast, that it took everyone, most of all Odwar, by surprise.

It felt like a volcano bubbling inside him. Every muscle in his body burned and stretched. His shadow exploded out of the ground and disappeared into his chest.

With the fly whisk still in hand, Odwar arched his

back and threw his arms wide. Something was building inside him, like lava rising up a quaking mountain.

Suddenly, his shadow erupted out of him. It was more violent than it had ever been. It roiled and seethed like a demon possessed as it churned around him.

Then, just as quickly as it had started, it stopped.

Nobody moved or spoke or dared to breathe.

Finally, after a few seconds of absolute stillness, the shadow began to take on a new shape. First four stout legs, then a muscular body, and finally a large animal-head and two massive horns.

Odwar's shadow settled into a form he had never seen it take before. The form of a bull.

You could have heard a feather drop as every eye gawked at the figure that had appeared in front of them. And when the shadow bull grunted, they all startled back. All of them, that is, except Odwar.

"Awesome," he whispered, chin trembling. He wasn't just referring to his shadow. *He* felt awesome too — bigger, stronger, braver. It was as if he had added one hundred pounds of muscle overnight. Odwar might have looked the same as he had a minute ago, but he certainly didn't feel the same. He felt *invincible*. All thanks to the fly whisk in his hand. His Entasim.

"Hand it over to me," Odwar's father ordered

suddenly, unfolding his palm. "I'll keep it for you until you're older. Until you're ready to have it."

"No," Odwar replied flatly.

His father's eyes bulged. Odwar had never refused a direct order from him before. "Excuse me?"

"It's mine. *My* Entasim. I'm not going to give it away. *Ever*." Odwar's awestruck eyes remained fixed on his shadow, not even bothering to look in his father's direction.

"You're only a child. You're not old enough to keep something so powerful."

"I SAID NO!" Odwar exploded.

At that moment, the shadow bull blasted out a bellow so loud that it seemed to shake the walls around them. Odwar could feel its power. Its rage.

"You always do this to me!" he railed. "You always make me feel like I'm not good enough!"

The shadow bull stomped one hoof on the ground and pointed its horns straight at his dad. Each heaving breath of the large animal matched Odwar's.

Dad's face twisted in confusion for a brief moment before he cleared his throat and calmly smoothed down his tie. "We'll talk about this tomorrow."

"No, we won't. I've got what I came here for. We're leaving for Nairobi first thing tomorrow morning."

"Odwar, you must—"

"*I. Said. No*," Odwar growled through clenched teeth. Then, without fully knowing why, he raised the fly whisk above his head.

Beside him, the bull charged forward a few steps, then stopped and looked back at Odwar. It was ready to attack and only awaited his command.

Odwar's father jumped back, his jaw slack with fear. "What are you...? You... I... We'll talk about this at home," he stuttered before backing down the stairs.

Odwar glared after him with his fist still tightly gripping the fly whisk. Molten determination rolled through him as he vowed to never let anyone take his Entasim away. It was *his*, and it was already making him braver than he had ever been.

"Odwar? Are you okay?" Soni asked, tapping his shoulder gently.

He flinched at her touch, then shrugged off his anger before turning to face her and the others. "Am I okay? I'm better than okay. I feel amazing!"

Xirsi tilted his head. "I think what she means is that we've never seen you talk to your dad like that."

"He deserved it," Odwar shot back.

Xirsi raised his hands in surrender. "Just saying... That was intense."

"Nobody is *ever* going to take this away from me." He twirled the fly whisk around in the air, drawing another bellow and stomp from the shadow bull. "This is exactly what I needed. I feel... I feel *powerful*... Like I can stand up to anyone and any*thing*. Even the Shadow Queen."

"Whoa, slow down a sec," Mwikali said. Her eyebrows were bunched together in worry. "I know what it's like to hold your Entasim for the first time. How exciting and scary and incredible it feels! How about you chill and, like, take it all in before going all attack-mode." She was clutching her belt bag, probably to still her rattling divining horn.

But Odwar didn't care what Mwikali, her Entasim, or anyone else thought. All that mattered was his orengo, and how it made him finally feel like the fierce warrior he had always wanted to be. "Attack-mode is exactly what we need to be in right now. Starting with that bodyguard ogre," he stated. "We're going to take him down and send a message to all the monsters of the underworld. We're going to let them know that the Intasimi Warriors are not afraid of them, and that we're stronger than we've ever been."

ODWAR VS. THE SHADOW QUEEN

The Intasimi Warriors vs. the Underworld

"Come on!" Odwar called out impatiently as he headed back outside and straight towards the large tent. "I'll draw him away from the other guests." He stuck out his tongue and waved mockingly at the ogre bodyguard to make good on his promise.

"Bro, I don't think this is such a good id—" Xirsi began.

"Too late!" Mwikali cried, sounding scared. "He's coming!"

Sure enough, with balled fists and a clenched jaw, the bodyguard had taken the bait and was stomping in their direction.

Odwar chortled hysterically as he whipped around and tore along the footpath to the animal pens.

"It's not funny!" Soni wheezed as they all chased after him.

But Odwar couldn't stop laughing. He didn't understand why his friends weren't enjoying this as much as he was. Didn't they get it? They were invincible now! They couldn't lose!

They came to a stop in the middle of the sheep and goat pasture. It was bordered by a long chicken coop on one side, a row of pig pens on the other, and a large cow shed right behind them.

They stood with their backs to each other, eyes darting around as they waited for the bodyguard to find them.

"So? What's the plan?" Xirsi panted while his fingers played an imaginary piano in the air.

"The plan is to teach him a lesson. To destroy him before he can go and report back to the Shadow Queen," Odwar answered.

"*Destroy* him?" Soni asked, frowning.

All three of them were staring at Odwar with pinched faces and downturned lips. He couldn't blame them. The words had come out of nowhere — they didn't even sound like his! In fact, Odwar was pretty sure he had never said the words "destroy him" in his life.

He was about to take it back when he spotted four large figures at the far end of the field. The bodyguard had finally arrived, and he had brought some friends along for the fight. Three paramilitary soldiers dressed in camouflage uniforms, leather boots and black berets marched alongside him. Odwar's heart leapt into his throat as the men stormed towards them.

Mwikali gasped. "Oh no, no, no..."

"Sorry, I didn't think he'd bring company," Odwar started to say, but Mwikali was shaking her head, her eyes as wide as dinner plates.

He knew that look. It was *the* look. "Are they all... ogres?" he guessed.

She opened her mouth but no sound came out. It was only when she put a hand over her eyes that she found the courage to speak. "The bodyguard is. But the army guys aren't. They're not ogres, they're...*worse*."

"What could be worse than ogres?" Soni wondered with a trembling voice.

Odwar looked from his friends to the men, and then back to his friends. *Why did you bring them here?* his brain screamed. *Why did you put them in danger?*

He swallowed his guilt and put a hand on Mwikali's shoulder. "Please, open your eyes and tell us what you see. Those three other guys... What *are* they?"

Mwikali slowly pulled her hand away. "They look like hyenas. Only, they're *monster* hyenas. Their eyes are empty dark holes, but there's a weird green light shining through each one. And they have huge heads with snapping, knife-like teeth."

"*Werehyenas*," Xirsi breathed. "They're half-human, half-hyena. Common in East and North Africa. Known to rob graves and eat dead bodies." He turned to his friends with a frighteningly grave expression on his usually cheerful face. "Guys, whatever you do, don't look them in the eyes. That's how they hypnotise their victims."

Soni groaned. "Hypnotising hyenas? Great. Just *great*. How on earth are we supposed to fight them without looking at them?"

"We're not gonna fight with our eyes," Odwar answered. "We'll fight with our powers. Remember when Mr Lemayian had us run practice drills while blindfolded? Just like that. Soni, your sense of hearing is out of this world — use it. Mwikali, you have your intuition. Xirsi, your animals. You guys deal with the werehyenas. And remember to keep your eyes *closed*. I'll handle the bodyguard ogre."

The four monsters were slowly closing the gap between them. And judging by their size, what they lacked in speed, they were sure to make up for in strength.

"Spread out," Odwar commanded. They quickly got into fighting positions, lining themselves up so each was paired directly across from a different monster.

"Alright, here they come!" Odwar shouted. "Close your eyes!"

THE INTASIMI WARRIORS VS. THE UNDERWORLD

They obeyed his command, and when the monsters attacked, he was the only one who saw it. The beasts hunched over and dropped their large arms down to the ground. They ran on all fours, looking more like animals than men.

Odwar pulled out the fly whisk from his back pocket. Instantly, his shadow bull materialised beside him. "Now!" he boomed at his friends, noticing that his voice sounded deeper than usual. It sounded remarkably similar to the bellowing shadow beside him. So much so, in fact, that he couldn't quite tell if it was him or the bull that had belted out the command.

Soni wasted no time. Planting her feet apart, she punched her hands forward and sent a blast of energy straight into the monster in front of her. He collided head on with the sonic wave and was immediately sent flying backwards as if he'd been hit by a speeding truck.

At the very same time Soni's werehyena was flailing helplessly through the air, another was getting mauled, pecked and bitten by all the creatures Xirsi had summoned. On his order, dozens of farm animals had stampeded out of their enclosures and into battle.

Mwikali, with eyes closed like the others, danced circles around her werehyena. Every time the beast lunged forward, she slid to the side. Every time he reached out to grab her, she ducked down. Odwar couldn't help but smile as he watched his friend, knowing full well that with her powers of prediction, the monster she was up against would never be able to get his hands on her.

Once he was sure that his friends were okay, Odwar turned to face his own nightmare — the ogre bodyguard. He trailed behind the werehyenas, swaying from side to side as he slogged forward.

Although he had never fought with his shadow bull before, Odwar could feel its mighty fury saturating the air around him. It made his skin prickle with anticipation.

He tightened his fist around the fly whisk and then shot it high into the air. On cue, the bull barrelled forward. It moved faster than he could ever have imagined, even faster than it did when it was just a whooshing black cloud.

It was on a collision path with the ogre, speeding closer to it...when the ogre twisted to the side at the last minute, but not before the bull's left horn clipped his shoulder and knocked him over.

Odwar clapped his hand over his mouth in surprise. His shadow had never been able to do that before. Actually *hurt* people. And now it could. In fact, with horns that large, it could do much more than hurt.

The ogre sat up, clutching his right arm. From the grimace he wore on his face, he looked to have landed too poorly to get up right away. The shadow bull came to a stop a short distance ahead and spun around to face the ogre once more. It snorted and stomped its hoof angrily, eager to continue, only waiting for the go-ahead to do so.

Odwar's heart throbbed with excitement. His whole body buzzed with an electrifying sense of strength. Strength he had always wished he had. A *warrior's* strength. It felt like he was at the centre of a boxing ring with the entire crowd cheering for him to give his opponent the final blow. Odwar's lips curled in a victorious smile as the ogre sat helplessly on the ground.

The shadow bull grunted once more and flicked its tail, waiting for permission to attack. The ogre was injured, no longer a threat, and Mr Lemayian had taught them to only attack in defence of themselves or others. There was no need to fight any longer. Even so, dark thoughts swirled around Odwar's mind. His hand trembled in mid-air. His fingers twitched, prompting the bull to aim its horns at the ogre in response.

"Odwar, NO!"

Mwikali's scream cut through the air, loosening his grip on the fly whisk. The shadow bull vanished as his

ODWAR VS. THE SHADOW QUEEN

Entasim fell to the grass. Odwar felt as if he had been knocked out of a trance.

Before he knew it, his friends were dragging him by the arms as they ran past, and he just managed to stuff the fly whisk into his pocket as they pulled him away.

"What were you thinking back there?" Soni demanded as soon as they were safely back in his bedroom.

Odwar dropped his eyes to his trainers, not knowing what to say. How could he possibly explain the feeling that came over him when he held his Entasim? He could hardly understand it himself. "I... I..."

KNOCK. KNOCK. KNOCK.

His grandmother pushed the door open and smiled warmly as she leaned against its frame. "The guests are leaving. Why don't you come say your goodbyes so we can sit down for some tea? I'm sure your friends would like that."

The tension in the room softened and faded away under the spell of Grandmother's calming voice. Her invitation was accepted enthusiastically with unanimous nods. "Oh, and Odwar, your father tells me that you found what you were looking for?" she added.

Odwar excitedly pulled the fly whisk out of his pocket. "Yeah! And you should see what I can do with this orengo, Dana. How powerful I am!"

She nodded and smiled knowingly. "Powerful, eh? And what exactly does that mean?"

He scrunched up his face, wondering why she would ask him something so obvious. "It means I'm *strong*. Stronger than I've ever been!"

His grandmother stepped back from the door with a half-quirked mouth. "True power isn't just about strength," she said, turning to walk away. "It's about compassion too. True power is about *balance*."

ODWAR VS. THE SHADOW QUEEN

Brothers vs. Uncle

Uncle Cyrus and his entourage of bodyguards trooped into the house shortly after the last guests had exited the compound. Settling into a large armchair, Uncle grinned approvingly as he feasted his eyes on the sumptuous treats spread out on the living room's coffee table. He leaned forwards eagerly and let his gaze roam the snack trays piled high with crispy samosas, puffy mandazis, plump sausages and spongy cakes. If not for one of his bodyguards drawing his attention away, Odwar was sure the man's greed would have tipped him over and sent him falling belly-first onto the floor.

It was the ogre. Glaring at the Intasimi Warriors the whole time, he stooped over while rubbing his shoulder and whispered in Uncle's ear. Then he pointed at the fake fly whisk resting on the armrest before retreating to the back of the room.

Every hair on Odwar's body stood straight up. His eyes flitted to his friends who were seated on the sofa beside him. Their darting eyes relayed a conjoined fear. A fear that doubled into panic when Uncle lifted the fly whisk and rolled it slowly in his palm under a scrutinizing gaze.

He knows! Odwar thought, terrified. *He knows it's not his orengo and he's going to kill me.*

"Odwar, are you okay?" Grandmother asked. Her quizzical expression matched that of Gor who was seated on the two-seater chair right next to her. Together, they eyed Odwar worriedly.

"I... I..." he spluttered, eyes moving back and forth between his grandmother and his uncle.

Uncle Cyrus continued to study his fly whisk. Mwikali, Soni and Xirsi shifted and shuffled nervously in their seats. Odwar could only stare at the scene unfolding in open-mouthed panic.

Gor leaned to the side and whispered something in his grandmother's ear. She turned to Uncle Cyrus, then to Odwar, swivelling her head back and forth between them one more time before facing Gor. A look of understanding passed between them. She pursed her lips and gave Gor a nod that seemed to say, "Do it".

He got up and strode towards their uncle.

"It's even more beautiful up close. Uncle Cyrus, it's always been a dream of mine to touch it. May I?"

Without waiting for a reply, Gor plucked the fly whisk from Uncle's hand and held it up to his eyes.

BROTHERS VS. UNCLE

"Magnificent. Sturdy, solid handle. I can't believe I'm finally holding it in my own hands!"

Grandmother joined Gor at their uncle's side. She placed one hand on Gor's shoulder and used the other to take the fly whisk from him. "Ah, yes. To wield an orengo is a great privilege. A privilege that can't be stolen or forced. A privilege that can only be given or earned. That's why only those with a true right to the orengo get to keep it."

Odwar's father, who was seated next to Uncle Cyrus, bowed his head at these words and, just for a split second, Odwar thought he saw a tear tremble in his eye.

A loud, forced laugh erupted from Uncle's lips. The kind of laugh that sounded embarrassed rather than happy. "More than anything else, what matters is the character of he who wields it. Not the orengo itself. It is, after all, a symbolic object." His smile was shaky and the look in his eyes desperate as he gawked at the fly whisk secured in Grandmother's small hand.

It was clear to Odwar what was happening. Gor had been paying more attention back in the tent than he had shown. He knew all about the heist. He had witnessed the fly whisk swap in progress. Then, right there in the living room, he had observed Odwar and understood his fear during the moments Uncle Cyrus was investigating the fake fly whisk. As soon as he relayed what he knew to their grandmother, they had resolved to get Odwar out of trouble.

Gor had gone in first with a distraction. Now, Grandmother was calling Uncle Cyrus out for stealing what should have rightfully belonged to Dad. She was questioning his very right to ownership of the fly whisk, and he couldn't accuse someone of stealing something that wasn't actually his! Besides, wasn't it the person who held the orengo who mattered and not the actual orengo itself?

RING. RING. RING.

Only Uncle Cyrus would have his phone set to the most loudly obnoxious ringtone on earth. He flipped the leather phone case open and barked a few words into the mouthpiece before rocking out of his seat.

"Polling results for the county just came in. I have to leave straight away for the party HQ," he announced.

As his bodyguards jumped into action, he extended an impatient hand towards his mother and beckoned for her to place his orengo in it. She remained absolutely still, making him wait for a few extra seconds before she planted it in his wide open palm.

All too quickly, Uncle Cyrus tossed it into his briefcase, and without so much as a goodbye, marched out of the house.

Grandmother locked eyes with Odwar's dad and then with Odwar. She held their gazes with such intensity that without saying a single word, with just a look, she let them know exactly how she felt: that the matter was settled, that the fly whisk — the real one — was exactly where it belonged.

Dad cleared his throat and knuckled something from his eye. "Gor, Odwar, go and tell them we're ready for tea."

It was a cue to seal the win and end the matter, and one the brothers were only too eager to comply with. Off to the kitchen they went, patiently waiting side-by-side as the kitchen staff pulled boiling pots of masala tea from the stove and poured it into large stainless-steel flasks.

"Thanks," Odwar said softly after they had stood together for a while. "For your help back there...with Uncle. Why did you do it, though? Help, I mean. Things between us haven't been exactly great since..."

"Since you became an Intasimi Warrior?" Gor sighed. "You're right. Getting over the fact that I wasn't the gifted one has been...hard. Dad drummed it into my head that it was going to be me for so long that when it wasn't, I didn't know who I was anymore. I felt...useless. But seeing you look so helpless back there with Uncle Cyrus, and even at breakfast the other day with Dad, made me realise that I do have an important role to play, and that that role is to be your big brother. And getting little brothers out of trouble is exactly what big brothers are for." Gor smiled and clapped Odwar on the back. "And Dana is right, by the way. The real orengo is yours by right. The Intasimi gift too — it was always meant to be yours. You were born for it. I'm happy and *proud* that it's you."

A feeling of warmth unfolded like a flower in Odwar's belly. The glint of emotion shining in his brother's eyes was proof that he truly believed the words he said. Gor's approval meant a lot to him. Almost as much as approval from...

A bitter thought brought Odwar crashing back to reality. "Dad wanted it to be you. I think he hates me because I remind him of Uncle Cyrus. You remind him of *him*. You're the first born. You're bigger, stronger... You're just like him. He'll never stop wishing it was you who got the gift."

A deep voice at their backs startled them both.

"Coffee," their father said huskily. "Don't forget to ask them to bring coffee as well."

Dad stood watching them, his broad shoulders and

tall frame filling the kitchen entryway entirely. Neither Gor nor Odwar had heard him approach and neither knew how long he'd been standing there or how much he had heard. But when he lingered for a moment too long, opening his mouth to speak and then closing it soundlessly, they both feared that he had heard a bit too much.

Their father retreated back to the living room without another word.

*

A yellow ball of fire unfolded before them, lighting each face and outshining the stars. Odwar, Soni, Xirsi and Mwikali sat close to the bonfire, allowing its heat to warm their cores as they watched golden sparks shoot into the starry black night.

"What story would you like to hear?" Odwar's grandmother asked, cradling a mug of bone broth in her hands.

Four voices erupted at once:

"How elephant got its trunk!"

"Why spider has eight legs!"

"The one about tortoise and hare!"

"When monkey tricked crocodile!"

The children nudged each other excitedly, not really minding which of their stories was picked. It was wonderful enough that they got to sit together by a toasty campfire and listen to a traditional folktale. Everyone knew that grandmothers were the best storytellers on earth and Odwar knew that his grandmother was the best storyteller of all.

The old woman settled back into her foldable safari green camp chair with a twinkle in her eyes. "Hmmm, I think I'm going to tell you the one about how leopard got its spots. Have you heard this one before?"

When the four friends shook their heads, Grandmother looked pleased. She took a long sip from her mug and shot Odwar a meaningful glance before closing her eyes.

Suddenly, she lifted her face into the dark night and began the story the way all stories had begun since the time her own grandmother was young, with a call to the listener:

"Hadithi, hadithi!" she cried out.

"Hadithi njoo!" the children called back dutifully.

"Story, story!" she repeated.

"Let the story come!" they replied again.

"Then let the night be quiet, and the story told. You see, boys and girls, leopard has always been powerful and wise, but she hasn't always been so unique and beautiful." Grandmother's voice was low and throaty, punctuated by the sounds of crackling flames. "No. There was a time when leopard had plain, ordinary fur. She wasn't striped like zebra, didn't have a glorious mane like lion, or the beautiful colours of peacock. Her fur was just that. Fur. Still! She held her head high because she knew that what made her truly beautiful was inside her.

"One day, as she was resting high up in the branches, she heard an animal crying down below. It was snake. Animal after animal passed alongside snake, one after the other, but they all scampered away. None dared to stop and ask poor snake what was wrong. They were all too afraid that snake would bite them. All that is, except leopard.

"You see, leopard knew that there were two sides to every story. She knew that every creature deserved to tell theirs. And so, she lowered herself from the tree and went to snake's aid. It turns out that snake had been crushed under the heavy foot of elephant. It was why he always snapped at the heels of other animals in the first place, so that they wouldn't trample him. This time, he hadn't seen elephant coming. Now, all he needed was to be carried back to his cave where he could heal.

"Leopard gently picked snake up and carried him

away to safety. And when snake was feeling better, he gave leopard a gift. A little bite on the tail that turned her fur into the magnificent spotted beauty it is today. And that is the story of how leopard got her spots."

Soni clapped her hands, beaming from ear to ear. "So, leopard got her pretty spots because she showed kindness to snake."

"Mmhmm. Many creatures respected leopard for her poise and power, but after that day, they respected her just as much for her *compassion*."

Odwar thought about the story of the leopard the next morning as they piled into the van that would take him and his friends back to Nairobi. He couldn't help but feel that his grandmother had narrated that particular story especially for him.

It was the last thing on his mind as the warm carriage of sleep swooped him up and whisked him away to another world.

Shadow Bull vs. Shadow Queen

The smell of mould, an eerie chill in the air and sounds of ghostly moaning had become familiar to Odwar. He had been in the shadow world enough times to expect them. What he hadn't foreseen was the red haze that now cloaked everything around him. It was the first thing he noticed when his eyes blinked open.

At first, he wondered if he was wearing those red-tinted sunglasses that Iron Man wore, but it wasn't until he reached for his face that he realised that something else wasn't right. He glanced down and immediately froze. In place of his hand was a hoof. In place of his human body was the stocky torso of a bull. He tilted his head side to side and felt the centre of gravity shift each time one of his large horns dipped down.

A shiver of wonder rippled from his thick neck right down to his cloven hooves, and a feeling of power pulsated in his muscles. He stomped, prompting an eruption of chitters from the shadow spawn on every side of him. The creatures, who now looked blood red through his bull eyes, whizzed around excitedly, whispering words in a language he couldn't understand. This was strange. They were usually sad and mournful. This new energy made Odwar's nerves tingle slightly. What was making them so happy?

It didn't matter. He was a bull. A shadow bull. *His* shadow bull. Nothing could scare him now, not even the shadow spawn nor their Shadow Queen.

As if the thought had summoned her, a gust of icy wind swiftly screamed past him, followed by a devilish laugh.

"Hello, my little shadow prince," came a familiar voice.

The blast of midnight purple air twisted and seethed around him for a little longer before pulling back and morphing into the Shadow Queen. Her form seemed to have doubled in size since the last time he saw it. Now she was four, maybe five times Odwar's height, her white eyes burning stories above his head.

"You're back," she purred, sounding a little bit too pleased for Odwar's liking. Didn't she see what he had become? How strong he now was?

I'll have to show her, he resolved. "MEUGHHHHHHH!"

The sound was deep, loud and shook all of his muscles as it rumbled out of his mouth. He had never bellowed before and was surprised at how

naturally it came to him. So he did it again. And again.
"MEUGHHHHHHH! MEUGHHHHHHH!"

"Is that the best you can do?" she mocked.

Odwar pawed at the ground and snorted as rage roiled inside him. "I'm not scared of you!" he roared.

This only made the Shadow Queen's shrill laughter ring louder through the darkness. "Oh, you are definitely scared. In fact, you are terrified. You call yourself a warrior but you're nothing but a terrified...little...*boy*."

He exploded into an angry gallop, determined to show her that he was *not* a boy. He was finally so much more. He was finally a warrior.

Bull-Odwar picked up pace until he was charging at full speed, directly towards the Shadow Queen who didn't flinch or try to get away. In fact, her laughter grew louder as he barrelled forwards.

Right before their collision, Odwar saw her grow a few feet taller. He heard the twittering from the shadow spawn turn into shouts of joy, and the Shadow Queen shriek in delight.

Right before their collision, it occurred to him that he had made a terrible mistake, that he was doing exactly what she wanted him to do. It dawned on him that he was playing right into her hands.

But by then it was too late.

He ploughed into her. But rather than come out on the other side, Odwar found himself entrapped at the epicentre of her twisting form. Dark vapours whipped around him at lightning speed, making it hard for him to move or even breathe. And when he looked down at himself, he saw that he was back in his human form.

Panic seized him immediately, turning his bones to water and his skin to ice. He wheeled around, searching frantically for his shadow, for a way out, but he couldn't find either. He opened his mouth to cry out for help, but in true nightmare fashion, no sound came out.

He was trapped.

Odwar trembled at the thought of being stuck in the shadow world forever. But just as that idea was eating away at his mind, he saw the outline of a figure moving in the windstorm — someone was out there.

He rubbed his eyes and squinted into the darkness once more. There she was again! It was a young woman, running. She was bald, dressed in brown animal hide, and looked to be only a few years older than Gor.

"Hey! Help! Help me!" he cried out to her, jumping up and down, waving his arms. But she couldn't hear him. She just kept running.

Where was she going? Was she trying to get away from the shadow world too?

SHADOW BULL VS. SHADOW QUEEN

The girl's eyes suddenly widened and her mouth split into the widest of smiles, right before she leapt into someone's arms. A young man, also wearing animal hide, was lifting her up and spinning her around. With both their heads thrown back, sounds of airy laughter filled the air.

Odwar frowned as he struggled to make sense of what he was seeing. The two weren't in the shadow world. Even though he could see them, they were in some other place, on a beach, with a large body of water shimmering behind them. A fleet of canoes bobbed on the lake carrying men who were all busily engaged in different kinds of fishing. Some pointed and hurled spear-like sticks, others held woven baskets in the shape of fishermen's hats underwater, while others sprinkled what looked like powder onto the water's surface and then scooped up the fish that bobbed up. A few feet from the water line, a crew of women sat sun-drying and selling fish brought in by the fishermen.

The canoes, the fishing and the Dholuo language he could hear in snatches of conversation all around him told Odwar where this scene was taking place — by the shores of Nam Lolwe. He knew it to be Africa's largest lake which bordered Kenya and the neighbouring countries of Uganda and Tanzania. The Savanna

Academy's former headmaster, whom they had known as Babu, had taught all the children at the school to use the lake's original name — Nam Lolwe — and not the one the colonisers had given it: Lake Victoria. It was one of the many lessons that the old man had instilled in them about cherishing culture before revealing himself to be the Red Oloibon and a super villain.

Judging from the traditional way everyone was dressed, Odwar could tell that they were not just in another place, they were most likely in another *time*. Something like this had happened to Mwikali when she had been transported back to an era when people still wore cow hides and goat skins. He was sure the same thing was happening to him now. But who were these people?

The couple continued to twirl in each other's arms, with eyes sparkling and faces glowing with delight. They were as happy as could be and Odwar felt an unexpected surge of joy swell inside him too, blooming as if it were his own. Sunshine flooded his heart and for a second he completely forgot where he was.

Then, before he could fully come to terms with what was happening, the couple jolted apart. Something had startled them. Odwar followed their panicked eyes to a gang of men. They were tramping towards the two with raised fists and angry shouts. His own heart drummed in his chest, making him feel just as scared as the couple looked.

The men were upon them in an instant, clobbering the young man with their bare fists and dragging the woman away from him. The young couple tried to resist, they tried to cling on to each other, but it was no use. They were no match for the gang who seemed determined to separate them. Not even gaping stares from the surprised fishing folk could stop them.

Raw anger shot through Odwar as he watched the woman being hoisted onto a shoulder. She pounded repeatedly on the back of her kidnapper as he carried her away. Tears streamed down her twisted face as she screamed for them to stop.

Something hot slid down Odwar's cheek too — tears. He could feel her emotions thrumming through his veins, quickening his blood, making him tighten his fists and scream so loudly that his throat burned. Her fear and anger overtook him completely, until it felt as if he was the one slung over someone's shoulder, being carried away.

"Odwar!"

The sound was faint, coming from somewhere above him. Someone was calling his name.

"Odwar!"

More than one person, *people* were calling his name. He recognised these voices! His friends! His friends were calling out to him.

He tore his eyes away from the young woman and looked up, where a pinhole of light had pierced through the darkness above. Was it a way out?

He blinked hopefully at the tiny bright star — once, twice — and when his eyes reopened the third time, he was back in the van.

"You're awake," Mwikali sighed, clutching her chest.

Odwar quickly sat up and took in the worried faces around him. "Guys, I'm fine."

"No, you're not. You had another nightmare, didn't you?" Soni demanded with crossed arms.

"This one looked pretty bad," Mwikali added.

"It wasn't! I wasn't even scared—" he started, but Xirsi cut him off.

"Bro, you were screaming just like the last time and... and..."

"And what?" Odwar asked.

Xirsi lowered his eyes. "And you were *crying*."

Odwar felt his face burn. He cleared his throat and spoke as confidently as he could. "I wasn't scared this time though. I took the Shadow Queen head on, rammed right into her. But then I started seeing this...this vision. *That's* why I was crying. There was this young woman and they were taking her away and... You know what? It doesn't matter. All that matters is that I'm not scared of the Shadow Queen anymore."

"That's not all," Mwikali said. Her brows were bunched together and she spoke as if she had to force the words out. "Your shadow was gone for most of the time you were asleep. And then, right at the end, it came back. But it looked...different. Tall, white eyes, long hands and claws. It looked like...like a *monster*."

Odwar's stomach did a flip when Mwikali proved her words with a phone recording of the whole thing. "The Shadow Queen," he whispered.

"She tried to get us! She was reaching and grabbing and everything, but it was like she was stuck to your body. That's when we started shouting for you to wake up," Soni said.

"I don't understand. How was she *here*?" Odwar muttered.

"I don't know, but *that*," Xirsi said, pointing at the fly whisk lying across Odwar's lap, "hasn't made things better. It's made them worse."

"No! You guys don't understand," Odwar argued. "I don't know what the vision meant or how the Shadow

Queen was able to get here, but I know the fly whisk made me strong enough to face her. I was a *bull*."

Even as he tried to convince his friends that his Entasim had changed the game by making him braver, a worrying thought gnawed at the edges of Odwar's mind. It had first occurred to him when Mwikali said that the Shadow Queen had appeared in the van. It lined up with the feeling of having made a mistake when he attacked her in the shadow world. He couldn't shake the idea that he had somehow given the Shadow Queen exactly what she wanted.

Odwar didn't dare share this fear with his friends. That would only prove that he was wrong and that they were right. It would mean that his fly whisk had made things worse instead of better. No. He had to figure this out on his own first...

"It's time to tell Mr Lemayian everything," Soni declared, backed by nods of agreement from Mwikali and Xirsi.

"Okay...we can tell him. But just give me this week to figure some things out on my own. We can tell him in a week, during our tutoring lesson," Odwar said, finally giving in.

They were back in Nairobi within the next half an hour, and once his friends had been dropped off at their homes, the van dropped Odwar at his. Once inside, he made sure his bedroom door was locked before raising his fly whisk and bringing his shadow bull to life. It snorted and flicked its tail, muscles trembling with ready anticipation. It brought Odwar's mind back to that moment when he charged at the Shadow Queen in bull form.

She had *wanted* him to do it — to lose his temper and go after her.

If what Odwar feared was true, the Shadow Queen wasn't trying to trap him in the shadow world.

She was trying to escape it.

ODWAR VS. THE SHADOW QUEEN

Boy vs. Shadow

Odwar felt a heaviness in his tummy as he walked into Savanna Academy after the break. The uneasy feeling only worsened when he spotted Mr Lemayian at the centre of the school quad wearing a playful grin that was framed by his distinct goatee and moustache combo. Mr Lemayian stood high-fiving a sea of uniform-clad students as they walked past him on their way to class.

With plum red locs and a sporty build, Mr Lemayian was the youngest headmaster that Savanna Academy had ever had, or at least, he looked to be. Odwar and his friends had only recently discovered that their mentor was immortal, which technically made him the *oldest* headmaster that Savanna Academy had ever had.

Mr Lemayian had taught the Intasimi Warriors everything they knew about being gifted descendants. On Saturdays, during private lessons held specially for them, he tutored the four warriors on Intasimi history so that they could better understand their gifts. He was turning them from ordinary kids into extraordinary fighters by guiding them as they sharpened their powers through practice.

During the half-day classes, he explained to them the dos and don'ts of being superheroes. Like, how important it was to keep their superpowers a secret from the world, because regular people feared what they couldn't understand. And how, as a perfect age-set, their team would always be stronger when they worked together.

The weight of the secret Odwar was keeping from Mr Lemayian felt like an anchor tugging at the pit of his stomach. Not telling his mentor about the nightmares or that he had found his Entasim felt wrong in every way possible, and yet...

Just one week, Odwar promised himself. *Just this one week to myself, alone with my Entasim. I'll tell him everything on Saturday.*

Even if he refused to admit it, a part of Odwar knew that the fly whisk had a hypnotising effect on him. When it was in his hand, he was under its spell and he wasn't always sure what he would say or do next. But he told himself that that was the exact reason he needed more time without anyone meddling. He would use the time to get better at commanding and learning how to control it.

Since their time in Kisumu, that's just what Odwar had done: wield his fly whisk, raise his shadow bull to life and delight in its power. He had hardly eaten or slept or even spoken to anyone during that time.

"Odwar!" Mr Lemayian called out, cheerfully waving him over.

A slick layer of sweat started to form under Odwar's shirt collar. His blazer suddenly felt too heavy, his tie too tight. Despite the chilly Nairobi morning, beads of sweat sprouted on his nose.

"Hi," he greeted the headmaster with a tight smile. He squeezed the straps of his backpack, all too aware that his secret, his Entasim, was inside it.

Mr Lemayian raised his palm to slap Odwar's. "How was your half term? Did you do anything interesting?"

Anything interesting? Odwar looked away and chewed the inside of his cheek as memories from the Kisumu trip swam through his mind: cutting the hairs off an angry bull, pulling off a heist to get Uncle Cyrus' fly whisk, having his shadow transform into a shadow bull, battling werehyenas and ogres...

"No," he choked out, the lie feeling like a spoonful of salt in his mouth. "It was pretty chill."

Mr Lemayian dished out more high fives to passing kids before turning back to Odwar. "Did you get a chance to hang out with the others over the break?"

"Yeah...a little. Kind of."

If Mr Lemayian had been paying attention, he would have noticed the unnaturally high pitch in Odwar's voice, and how he kept rubbing his palms against his trousers. He would have caught Odwar in his lie. But, fortunately for Odwar, as a newly appointed headmaster, Mr Lemayian had to deal with a lot more stuff. Like the rowdy gang of boys with missing ties that had just bumbled into the quad.

Odwar managed to slip away quietly as Mr Lemayian drifted off to deal with them and he breathed a sigh of relief when he was safely in class and settled at his desk. With all his new responsibilities, Mr Lemayian was sure to be distracted for the rest of the week. He had a good chance of not having to confess the truth until Saturday.

"Did you notice something weird about Mr Lemayian?" Soni asked the minute she plopped down onto her chair.

"What do you mean?" Odwar worried that he might not have got away with his lie after all.

"I'm not sure. He just seemed a little...I don't know... different."

"Are you guys talking about Mr Lemayian?" Mwikali joined in. She had just walked into class with the crowd of kids who got picked up and dropped off by the school's minibuses.

Soni nodded, scrunching her face. "Yeah, did you catch it too? Something's weird about him."

"Something like what?" Odwar asked again, fear tightening his chest.

Mwikali bobbed her head. "Yeah, and I think I know what it is. This is going to sound weird but... Mr Lemayian seems...older."

Odwar slumped back into his chair in relief. His secret was safe...for now. But, wait, did Mwikali just say older? How could Mr Lemayian be getting older if—

"He's immortal," Xirsi said, draping his sling bag over the back of his seat. "So he can't have grown older than he was before."

Soni had a serious look on her face as she slowly shook her head. "No, guys, Mwikali is right. That's what's different about him! The lines on his face, the way he moves a little slower now... Mr Lemayian is *aging*."

Wheels started to turn in Odwar's head. "Could it be because of the Forbidden Mask?"

Xirsi suddenly jerked up, his eyes flashing wildly as he snapped his fingers. "That makes sense! If Mr Lemayian was given immortality so he could finally destroy the Forbidden Mask, then it would mean that when the mask was finally destroyed—"

"His immortality would be taken away!" Soni

shouted, finishing his sentence.

They fell silent as each of them remembered how only a couple of months before, they had hunted down and destroyed an ancient mask — a weapon that the Red Oloibon, posing as the school headmaster, had hoped to use to open a door to a monster-filled underworld. Mr Lemayian had been there centuries before when the mask had first been formed and had been left on earth to make sure it was destroyed. Destroying the mask had sealed the monsters in the underworld forever and sent most of the ones who were already on earth into hiding.

"Do you think he knows? That he's...dying?" Odwar asked, feeling ten times worse that he was keeping a secret from their teacher and guide.

Mwikali hummed a yes. "I think so. He's probably just waiting for the right time to tell us. He promised never to keep secrets from us, remember?" She fixed her eyes on Odwar and raised her eyebrows. "Right before he asked us not to keep secrets from him."

Odwar scratched the back of his head and tried to ignore the hint of accusation in her voice and the guilt worming through his heart. "Yeah, speaking of that, let's meet in the field at break time for a little show and tell. I have something I want you guys to see."

BOY VS. SHADOW

*

Soni was the first to make it to the sports field. Barely two minutes after the bell rang for morning break, Odwar found her bouncing on her toes as she waited for him. He wasn't at all surprised.

Soni had been the first to have a gift awaken, and the first to learn everything there was to know about her bloodline's history. Her goal? To be perfect. Odwar wasn't sure if it had to do with the fact that she was the first-born kid out of three, or whether it was because her Intasimi ancestor was known for being one of a kind — the first female warrior in her community. Whatever the reason, Soni worked hard to be the best that she could be at *everything*.

"Hurry up!" she called out to him from the edge of the Mugumo Groves. The wooded area hulked behind her at the far end of the sports field and was rumoured to be cursed. The four friends knew that the groves weren't actually bewitched, not unless you were an evil spirit. So they took advantage of the fact that other kids avoided it and met there whenever they needed the privacy to practise their powers.

"It took you long enough," Soni said, grinning. "Mwikali has to work on something for Arts & Crafts club and Xirsi got pulled into a meeting with the football coach. So, it's gonna be just us."

"Oh," Odwar said, feeling a pang of disappointment. Then, seeing the eager twinkle in Soni's eyes, he remembered that she would have been the most excited to see his newfound control over his shadow bull anyway.

She led the way into the groves, and once they reached their usual spot in the middle of a small clearing, dropped down onto the grass. "Well? Let's see it!"

With pride streaking through him like a comet, Odwar took out his fly whisk and held her eyes for a moment. Just like his, they were wide with excitement, like the look on a kid's face right before a fireworks display goes off.

When he was sure she couldn't take the suspense anymore, he threw his hand into the air with a flourish and...

Nothing happened.

He looked all around him for any sign of his shadow bull and, finding none, tried again. This time, he pumped his fist hard, like he was delivering an undercut blow to an imaginary opponent.

Still, no shadow appeared.

Odwar noticed that Soni's expression had turned to one of confusion and smiled nervously before punching his fly whisk into the air over and over again.

"Come on!" he screamed at the top of his lungs. "Come out! I command you to come out!"

This had never happened to Odwar before. He was always able to summon his shadow. Even when it had been bound to the ground and looked like an ordinary boy, his shadow had always listened to him. What had changed?

Odwar glanced at his Entasim and felt a touch of fear as the unwelcome answer came to him.

"Hey, look, it's okay," Soni said, standing up. "You just have to practise a bit more. I'm sure you'll get the hang—"

"It's not okay!" Odwar barked. "I could do it before... Why won't it... Arghhh!" he growled, shaking his fly whisk angrily.

Soni took a worried step forward. "Dude, chill. It's really okay..."

"Stop saying that! You know what? Just forget about it. Leave me alone." With his face on fire, he stomped out of the groves.

The truth was that, more than anything, Odwar was embarrassed. Of all people to epically fail in front of, why did it have to happen in front of Soni? The Intasimi Warrior who had all but mastered her abilities?

His shadow drifted on the ground in step with him as he crossed the field. Just as he cast an angry glance in its direction, the shadow twisted itself into a frighteningly familiar shape. A spiky head with glowing oblong eyes looked up at him.

"Scared, *useless* shadow prince," it whispered menacingly. "Even weaker than you were before. Not a match for me *then*. Definitely not a match for me *now*."

Terror sent Odwar bolting at full pace out of the sun and into the school building.

What was happening to him?

The Intasimi Warriors vs. Odwar

"You snitched?" Odwar asked, glaring at Soni.

Mr Lemayian stepped in between them with lifted hands, palms outwards. "Now, now, Odwar. She was just worried about you. We all are."

"But there's nothing to worry about," he retorted. "I've got everything under control."

Odwar knew from the moment he walked into their Intasimi tutoring class on Saturday that his secret was already out. It was the way Mr Lemayian looked at him, with his lips pressed tight and eyebrows bunched close. That look of worry told him everything.

"Really, there's nothing wrong with me. It's taking me a little while to figure out my Entasim but I have it under control. I'm *fine*."

He dropped his eyes as he spoke the last words, knowing full well that he was anything but fine. There was a lot he wasn't telling them. Like how his shadow would occasionally take the form of the Shadow Queen. Like how he would catch glimpses of her on the ground beneath him, out of the corner of his eye, and sometimes even in his own mirror reflection.

He also hadn't told them that the nightmare from the van had returned. The one where he lost his cool and rushed the Shadow Queen, then got stuck in her vortex of visions. Every time, as he watched the young woman get kidnapped, her anger poured into him, becoming his own, until he woke up screaming with rage.

Soni let out a frustrated sigh. "Odwar, you're not in control. Something's going on with your Entasim and you know it."

Yes, Odwar was scared about all the changes that were happening with him but he was frustrated too. First his father and now his friends? Did everyone think he was too weak to do this? To handle the power of his Entasim? To be a warrior? He just needed some more time to get it right...

Mwikali's gasp scattered his thoughts and he turned to find her pointing at the space beside him where his shadow bull had just appeared. Without realising, he had pulled his fly whisk out of his pocket and was halfway through raising it. The bull was already on edge, snorting and glaring at his friends.

Odwar couldn't believe it. After several days of absence, his shadow bull was finally back!

"It's okay," he said, smiling as he returned his Entasim

into his backpack. But Mwikali didn't look okay. In fact, something in her eyes told him that she knew *he* wasn't okay either.

Mr Lemayian cleared his throat and reached for the rotary telephone on his desk. "Enough. Let's go down and begin today's lesson. We're going to learn about Odwar's Entasim — the orengo."

The four walked over to the grey sofa that sat in Mr Lemayian's office, but rather than settle down on it, they lifted the chair and pulled it back to reveal a trapdoor underneath. Mr Lemayian dialled one final number on the old-school dial-up phone and the door on the floor popped open, inviting them to descend into the room hidden in the basement.

It seemed like only yesterday that Odwar and his friends had discovered the secret passage to their mentor's underground office. Since then, he had allowed them to have their Saturday lessons in the concealed room. With its regal African decor and shelves lined with antique weaponry, it was the perfect setting for the Intasimi Warriors to learn about their special heritage.

Once inside and attentive in their seats, Mr Lemayian turned on the large screen mounted on the wall. An image of a fly whisk, much like Odwar's, appeared. It had long brown hairs flowing from a thick wooden handle.

"The fly whisk has been a treasured symbol of power across many communities in Africa," Mr Lemayian began, pointing a laser at the screen. "In the Luo community, it's called the orengo, and only a select few are allowed to carry it. When waved in the air, it can signal peace or war, respect or defiance, life or death, all depending on the emotions of the one who wields it."

A video then played of a funeral for an elder of a Luo village. A troupe of men were performing what was known as the Tero Buru dance where they dressed up in traditional costumes, wore masks and acted like they were fighting and chasing away evil spirits from the burial site. Afterwards, a man at the funeral rose up and waved his fly whisk in the air.

"See how he's waving his orengo around his head slowly like that? He'll do it six times in front of the casket to show his utmost regard for the deceased. It's the highest form of appreciation and respect you can show another person."

He went on to click through different fly whisks, some with white hair, others with brown, and a few with black hair like Odwar's. Some handles were nothing but thin, bumpy sticks while others were stocky, elaborately beaded works of art. Mr Lemayian showed them photographs of different historical figures waving their fly whisks; even the first president of Kenya, Mzee Jomo Kenyatta, carried one around with him.

Finally, he turned to Odwar with concern written on his brow. "Your Entasim is powerful enough to bring out the best in you...or the worst. It's meant to draw out whatever is inside you, making it stronger. We just have to make sure that it draws the right things out. That it doesn't turn you into someone you're not."

Odwar's throat tightened with memories of seeing the Shadow Queen appear in his reflection. "That's not gonna happen. I've got it under control," he repeated. His voice had a slight tremble to it and he hoped no one detected it.

Mr Lemayian's eyes lingered on him a little longer, and just as Soni opened her mouth to say something, the teacher stood up with a loud clap of his hands. "Time for power practice! I can't wait to see your shadow bull in action, Odwar."

Odwar could feel Soni's gaze still on him as they walked out of the underground office and into the Mugumo Groves. Xirsi and Mwikali whispered something to each other right before they spread out into a wide circle in the clearing. They were all studying him fearfully, wondering if he would be able to control his shadow bull. The fact that they all doubted he could handle the responsibility of his own Entasim brought back his edge of irritation and toughened his resolve to prove otherwise.

I'll show them, he thought as he gripped the fly whisk.

"Remember, this is a sparring session, so keep your attacks safe. We're not trying to hurt anyone. This is about practising your powers by pitting them against each other," Mr Lemayian instructed. Then he plunged a red flag into the ground at the centre of their circle and walked a safe distance away. "First one to capture the flag, wins. Go!"

Soni was the first. She was *always* the first. Her outstretched palms sent identical sonic waves straight at Mwikali and Odwar, causing both to stumble backwards and onto their bottoms. She took off in a sprint thereafter, heading straight for the flag, and had gone several yards when a swarm of locusts descended upon her out of nowhere.

Xirsi had obviously counted on Soni's quick reflexes and silently made the call out to the insects. Everyone knew that Soni *hated* bugs. Her immediate reaction was to crouch down on the ground and cover her ears.

"GROSSSSSSS!" she screamed.

Odwar quickly crawled over to where his fly whisk had dropped and hoisted it in the air. The shadow bull obediently sprung to life, and without wasting a moment, charged at the flag.

Mwikali — who had by now scrambled to her feet — and Xirsi raced after it but stopped short when the animal turned around menacingly and bellowed at them. Frozen in fear, they watched as the bull reached the flag and started to circle it protectively.

Odwar hopped off the floor and sauntered towards the waiting flag. "I win," he smirked.

"Oh no, you don't," Xirsi shot back, inching forward with raised hands. "Not yet. You have to pick up the flag with your *own hands* to win."

Odwar narrowed his eyes at his friend, seeing the glint in Xirsi's brown eyes, knowing exactly what he was about to do — summon insects or some other creatures from the animal kingdom to attack him.

He knew that he had to act fast, had to secure his victory. He could have just raced to the flag and grabbed it, but that wouldn't be enough. He wanted to prove once and for all that he was in complete control. To show them that his Entasim had made him a better, stronger warrior.

Odwar dropped his arm, and then shot his fist back up into the air. He did it so hard, so fast, that it looked like he was trying to punch a hole in the clouds.

The shadow bull leaped into action, galloping

headlong towards Xirsi who stood with widened eyes, rooted to the spot, not wanting to turn his back on the bull.

Somewhere in the distance Odwar heard Mwikali scream and Mr Lemayian yell for him to stop. He ignored them and kept his fly whisk in the air, eager to demonstrate that he could maintain control to the very end.

The bull was closing the gap fast. Its head was dipped, so that two large horns were aimed squarely at Xirsi's chest. In mere seconds, it would make impact. In 3... 2...

VOOOOOOOOOM!

A blast of sound, louder than a thousand bass horns, exploded all around. The kind of sound that could rip a hole in your eardrum.

Odwar fell to his knees and clapped his hands over his ears, not caring when his fly whisk tumbled to the ground and disappeared out of sight, along with the shadow bull. He curled his body into itself and waited for what seemed like hours for the roar of the horn to fade away.

Finally, when it did, he dared to drop his hands and look for the source of the sound. "Wh— What?" he stammered when he found out what and who had made the sound.

There, in front of him, stood Mwikali. Her divining horn was inches away from her lips, her chest heaving from the exertion of blowing it.

"How did you...? When did you...?" Odwar's brain was jammed. He had never seen Mwikali do anything like that. He hadn't even known the divining horn could make such a noise!

But before he could get any answers, Mr Lemayian yanked him up. "What were you thinking?" he boomed. "You could have seriously hurt Xirsi. Or worse!"

Odwar shook his head. "But we were all attacking each other. They did it too!"

"Not like that! Unlike you, none of them used brutal force. Soni could have pumped out a deadly sonic blast in her attack, but she didn't. Xirsi could have summoned killer bees instead of locusts — he didn't. And just now? Mwikali could have amped her horn all the way up to max and boiled your insides, *but she didn't.* Only you, Odwar. Only *you* took it too far."

"I wasn't going to go through with it... I wasn't going to hurt him..." he said weakly, unsure of his own words. The truth was, he couldn't be sure of anything. All he knew was what he felt when he lifted his fly whisk: raw, irresistible power.

"Yeah, right!" Soni scoffed. "If Mwikali hadn't stopped

you, you were *totally* going to smash into Xirsi."

Odwar shook his head again, switching his gaze from Soni to Mwikali and finally to Xirsi, who still looked as stunned as a deer in headlights.

"I think you better hand that over to me," Mr Lemayian ordered, pointing at the fly whisk.

"No!" Odwar cried out, scooping it off the ground and hugging it to his chest.

"Please, Odwar. It's changing you," Mwikali pleaded. "There's a darkness in your shadow now... An evil."

"You're not taking this away from me," he insisted, slowly pulling away. "You guys don't understand. It's made me stronger."

"It's made you *angrier*," Mr Lemayian corrected. "And with everything that's going on with your nightmares — with the shadow world — I don't think it's a good idea for you to hang onto something so powerful and... unpredictable."

Resentment rose inside Odwar like a tide, sending bitter thoughts pulsing through his mind. Nobody thought he was good enough to keep his Entasim — not his dad, not his mentor, nor his friends. They didn't think he was good enough to be an Intasimi Warrior.

"This is *my* Entasim, *my* birthright. And you will NEVER take it away from me!" he yelled.

And with his shadow bull galloping beside him, he turned and ran — away from his friends, away from his mentor, away from everyone who threatened to take his most prized possession away.

ODWAR VS. THE SHADOW QUEEN

Odwar vs. the Shadow Queen

Exhaustion weighed down on Odwar as he trod up to his bedroom that afternoon. Sparring with his friends had left him feeling drained. Sleep pulled at his eyelids as he swung his door open, and by the time his head hit the pillow, he was already in the other place, the shadow world. He was already in bull form.

His irritation crackled at the familiar sights and sounds. He was not in the mood for this. Not today.

"I know what you want!" he bellowed into the darkness. Startled shadow spawn skittered away from his voice and retreated further into the howling abyss.

He flicked his long black tail. "I know what you want and you're never going to get it! You're never getting out of here!"

This time, brittle laughter dripped like acid all around. The Shadow Queen. Her unbridled glee told him that she didn't care that he had figured out her plan. Didn't think he had it in him to stop her. Just like everyone else.

A riot of thoughts ran red through his brain, blinding

him to the shifting world around him. He hardly saw the vortex of dark-coloured vapours slowly forming. He didn't notice that his shadow bull was slowly separating from his human form.

"Did you hear me?" he raged. "I said you're never going to win. You're *never* getting out of here!"

"I ALREADY HAVE!"

The black whirlwind dropped at the sound of the Shadow Queen's voice, and Odwar had to shield his eyes from the sudden burst of light that followed her words.

It took a few blinks for his surroundings to come into focus. He saw his bed, gaming desk, football wallpaper — his room. He was out of the shadow world.

But right before the sigh of relief blew out of his chest, he saw something else. Something terrifying unfolding right in front of him.

His shadow bull was writhing in the air above his bed, jerking and thrashing, moaning as if in pain, as if begging for help. Odwar hopped up and stretched out his fingers as high up as they could go, but the bull was closer to the ceiling than to him.

He swiped his fly whisk off the side table and waved it around, cried "Stop!" but nothing worked.

After what seemed like a lifetime of agony, the bull grew grimly still. Then, slowly, its form started to change. Its muscular body stretched, its horns disappeared, its legs merged into two long arms with claws that touched the ground. A jagged head with bright flaming eyes emerged from the swirling black fog.

The Shadow Queen. Not only had she broken out of the shadow world, she had taken over his own shadow.

"What— What's happening?" he gasped.

Fear, confusion, shock, all circled inside Odwar.

Her eyes narrowed to thin slits; her voice deepened to a growl. "First, I'm going to wipe Lwanda's entire lineage off the face of this earth. Starting with you. And then? I'm going to invite those hidden in the shadows to claim your world as their own."

"You mean to fill it with hate, misery, fear and darkness! I won't let that happen!" shouted Odwar desperately.

The Shadow Queen reached out one long arm and scratched a claw against the ceiling. Dark green mould immediately began to spread from the spot she had touched. Veins of blight crawled along the stone and seeped down the beige walls. They slithered along the parquet floor and onto the furniture, covering everything in greenish black streaks. Odwar realised that the Shadow Queen was making good on her threat. She was turning his bedroom, his world, into the shadow world.

"Stop!" he cried out as fingers of mould snaked up his legs. Up and up they went, slipping into his mouth and in between his teeth. The musty stink filled his throat, making him gag.

The Shadow Queen rolled back her head and laughed. "You don't have the power to stop me, boy. This world was stolen from me and I intend to make it my home once more. Soon, everything here will be as it is in the shadow world. Soon, I'll be stronger than you could ever imagine."

A stab of hope pierced through Odwar's panic, silencing his jumbled thoughts. Did she say "soon"? *Soon* she would be stronger than he could imagine? He clung to the thought. Maybe it wasn't over yet. Maybe he still had time to stop this.

He looked down at his hand, then back up at the Shadow Queen. A sense of knowing settled over him. She had consumed his shadow, which meant that it — his shadow — was still in there...somewhere. And if that were true, then getting rid of her would be as easy as...

Odwar let the fly whisk slip from his palm.

In an instant, she was gone.

*

The next morning couldn't come soon enough. Odwar threw on a grey tracksuit and hurriedly stuffed his fly whisk into his backpack before bolting out of his room. Even though it was a Sunday, his friends had agreed to an emergency meeting in Mr Lemayian's secret office. There was no time to waste. He needed to talk to them before it was too late.

He tapped his foot impatiently in the dining room as he waited for the driver to come around. Mum was still asleep, jet-lagged from her most recent business trip, while Dad had travelled for an out of town meeting the day before. Gor was the only family member awake, and he stumbled into the dining room just as Odwar glanced at his watch for the millionth time.

"You okay?" he slurred, rubbing sleep away from his eyes and slumping into a seat. "And where're you going so early on a Sunday?"

Odwar kept his eyes trained on the window, wishing the driver would hurry up and get there. "Everything's fine. I just have something I need to do."

"Everything's *not* fine," Gor countered. "You haven't been 'fine' since Kisumu. You hardly come out of your room, barely touch your food... Something's been off with you ever since you got *that*." He pointed at the fly whisk.

Odwar shifted uncomfortably, twisting away so that his backpack and Entasim were out of Gor's view.

"I've got it under control," he said, crossing his arms defensively.

Gor was quiet for a bit and when he spoke, his tone was soft. "You know, it's okay to ask for help. To ask *me* for help."

In that moment, looking into his brother's eyes, Odwar was hit by a reminder of the bond they had once shared. His brother had always protected him, always been there for him. He longed to offload the burden of emotions weighing on his mind — fear of releasing the Shadow Queen into the world, shame at not being warrior enough to wield his Entasim, and finally, confusion about whether his fly whisk was making things better or worse. In that moment he longed to open up about how scared he really was and for his big brother to get him out of trouble like he always had.

But just as he opened his mouth to speak, a car horn blared outside. It snapped him out of his thoughts and clamped his mouth shut. Bitter memories began to overwrite the fond ones. This was Gor, the one who everyone thought should have been the Intasimi Warrior. The one who was stronger than him in every way. He couldn't let him — *them* — know just how right they were.

"I have to go," he announced, striding towards the door.

Gor followed him down the steps. "Odwar, wait! You can talk to me about whatever's going on. I'm worried about you…"

The car was ready and revving in the drive. "I said I'm fine," Odwar hurled back, sliding into the passenger side.

Gor's face clouded with concern. "I don't think you are…" he began. But Odwar had already slammed the car door shut in his face.

*

The ride to school was quick, and when he stepped out of the car and into the light of day, Odwar realised that it was the first time he had been outside since the sparring session. Having kept his curtains drawn all of the previous day, it was also going to be the first time he had seen his shadow since it had morphed into the Shadow Queen in his bedroom.

He peeped at it while crossing the empty school car park, worried what it would look like, terrified when his worst fears were confirmed. His shadow wasn't his anymore, at least not completely. It swirled about on the pavement underneath him, changing from bull form one second to Shadow Queen the next. It was as if she was trying to claim it entirely but wasn't quite strong enough. At least not yet.

Odwar broke into a run. He had to get out of the sunlight and into Mr Lemayian's office. It was the only way to stop whatever was happening — no light meant no shadow, and no shadow meant no Shadow Queen. For a brief second, he considered making a run for the Mugumo Groves, an area guarded against evil beings, but he knew he would never make it in time. Not with a wide, sun-bathed stretch of field to get across first.

As if sensing what he was thinking, his shadow whooshed up from the ground and raced after him, contorting wildly as it moved through the air, struggling to keep form, to resist the Shadow Queen.

"I've already won," a voice hissed from deep inside the cloud of vapours.

Odwar pushed harder, running so fast through the quad that he thought his legs were going to explode. As his terror swelled, so did his shadow. As his fear mounted, it scaled higher and higher into the air, looking more and more like the Shadow Queen.

The moment he burst into Mr Lemayian's office, a set of long claws reached out of the twisting fog to grab him, just managing to scratch his heels.

Once inside, with his back pressed against the door and his lungs and calves on fire, Odwar closed his eyes and fought to catch his breath.

"Odwar?"

He recognised the sound of Mwikali's voice but couldn't bring himself to open his eyes just yet. Adrenaline was coursing through his veins, making it hard to breathe or even think.

She called out to him again, urgently, in her *I-see-a-monster* voice.

"ODWAR!"

His eyes flew open and straight to his feet, where she — along with the others — were pointing.

A thick layer of mould coated his white high tops. And streaks of it were wriggling up his legs.

At that moment, a whistling sound by the door stole their attention and they turned to watch as blackish blue vapours streamed into the room from a thin gap under the door.

"Into the basement!" Mr Lemayian ordered, slamming down the receiver of his rotary phone.

Soni was already at the trapdoor and lifted it to let everyone through before hopping down into it herself.

In the dimly lit underground office, Odwar looked

down at his thighs. The mould was still there, but had stopped clawing up his body. "She... She's taken over my shadow," he whimpered to himself.

He told them everything that had happened since they were last together, and when he was done, he held his face in his hands. "How do I fight her? How do I get my shadow back?"

"You don't," Mr Lemayian said firmly.

Odwar's head jerked up. "What do you mean? There has to be a way I can—"

"You've done enough," Xirsi blurted out impatiently.

Soni pointed at a drawing that Mwikali was now holding up. It showed the three of them — Mwikali, Soni and Xirsi — fighting against a trio of shadows: a bull, the Shadow Queen...and a boy.

The shadows — *his* shadows — looked like monsters with eyes that burned bright against vapours of dark blue.

"Can't you see?" Soni said, still pointing at the open page. "*You're* the one we're up against, Odwar. You're the one we have to fight!"

Fight vs. Freeze

"I would *never* turn on you," Odwar bristled. "I would never hurt you guys!"

"Umm," Xirsi sang with raised eyebrows. He was pointing at himself, hinting at the time Odwar's shadow bull had almost flattened him.

"So you're saying that *I'm* the enemy now?" Odwar asked, voice thick with hurt.

Upstairs, the office door blew open with a bang as what sounded like a windstorm swept into the room.

"What we're saying," Mr Lemayian cut in, his voice deliberately calm, "is that until we know what's going on, it's best if we take every precaution we can." His eyes shifted to Odwar's backpack. To the fly whisk.

Odwar put a protective hand over his Entasim. "Why is everyone trying to take this away from me?"

The winds in the room above them screamed, whipping and slamming furniture against the walls.

"Everyone except the Shadow Queen!" Mwikali yelled, looking up worriedly as she took a step towards Odwar. "Have you wondered why? If it's the one thing you need to defeat her, have you ever wondered why she hasn't tried to take it from you?"

With his hand still guarding the side pocket of his backpack, Odwar took a step back. "Nobody asked you to give up *your* Entasim," he argued.

The ceiling groaned, sagging downwards under the pressure of whatever was ripping the office above them apart.

Mwikali took another step forwards. Her eyes shone with tears and she held her hands to her heart as she spoke. "My Entasim doesn't feed off energy like yours does. Odwar, I know something is wrong with you because I can *see* it. You're carrying around…I dunno… like, *bad vibes*. I can literally see them all around you. A dark haze has been following you everywhere. It looks all smoky and feels like fear and hate and anger, all mixed up in one."

Soni nodded so hard that her hair buns bounced. "It's probably what's been making you so snappy."

"I'm snappy because no one thinks I'm strong enough to control my own Entasim!" The raging sounds above mirrored the bitterness churning inside him and, try as he might, he couldn't bring himself to take in what his friends were saying. It felt like they were ganging up on him. He wondered bitterly if they had met beforehand to plan what they would say to him.

Xirsi stepped forwards with a hand pointed at the ceiling. "Listen to what's happening up there! You and the Shadow Queen — it's like you're connected somehow."

"Tethered," Mr Lemayian corrected. "She's tethered to you. It took me some time to figure it out, but...the Shadow Queen feeds off anger, hate, pride, terror — 'bad vibes' as Mwikali calls them. She feeds off these negative emotions, growing stronger every time she does. She was able to pull you into the shadow world because your shadow self is an actual physical thing, unlike other people's. Then she was able to consume your fear and anger...latching onto you and pulling herself into our world."

Soni marched across the zebra-print carpet towards Odwar, pointing angrily at the fly whisk. "And that thing makes it worse. It makes it easier for her to link herself to you, by making you proud and hateful and—"

"And stronger!" Odwar yelled, backing into the wall so that he stood between the world and his Entasim. "It's also given me a shadow bull and *made me stronger!* Don't you see? All I need to do is figure out how to control it... Then I know I'll be able to stop her!"

Screeching laughter swelled above the sounds of

destruction, and the ceiling sank even lower, threatening to cave in at any moment.

Odwar was so blinded by his desperation that he didn't notice that his friends had backed him into the furthest corner from the trapdoor. Nor that Mr Lemayian had pulled a spear from his weapons display shelf.

"Now!" Soni shouted, before spinning on her heels and racing towards the stairs. The others were right behind her, and before Odwar knew what was happening, they had shot up and out of the underground office, locking the trapdoor shut behind them.

He had been left behind. Trapped.

He had been tricked. *Betrayed*.

Fury roared through his body as he reached a quivering hand towards his Entasim. The idea that his friends didn't trust him squeezed at his chest as he drew the fly whisk out of his backpack. What happened to being stronger together? What happened to being a team?

They had left to fight the Shadow Queen without him, as if he was useless. As if he wasn't one of the Intasimi Warriors.

Well, he was going to have to show them that he could do it. He *could* control his fly whisk and join the

FIGHT VS. FREEZE

fight against the Shadow Queen. He *could* be an Intasimi Warrior.

He *was* an Intasimi Warrior. And whether they liked it or not, they needed him if they were going to win this fight.

Odwar balled a hard fist around the handle of his fly whisk, paused for a breath, and then jabbed the air with it.

WHOOSH!

He was suddenly upstairs. But not *really* upstairs.

He couldn't feel his body, because he had none.

He was nothing but a small cloud. A wisp of vapours. A formless shadow.

Somehow, his body had been left behind in the underground office and a part of him — the last remaining bit of shadow he had left — had escaped. He could still feel his physical body somewhere down below, frozen like a statue with the fly whisk held high, while his shadow was now hovering close to the ceiling in the room above.

The office was a wreck. Broken furniture lay splintered all around. Shards of window glass were stabbed into the wall, while ripped up pages of books carpeted the floor. It was as if a bomb had been detonated right in the centre of the room.

ODWAR VS. THE SHADOW QUEEN

What was left of shadow Odwar remained suspended and unnoticed as several things below him unfolded at the same time.

Mr Lemayian stood protectively on top of the trapdoor with his legs spread wide apart, waving around the spear retrieved from his shelf. His movements were slow, and with his bird's eye view, Odwar saw for the first time what his friends had seen earlier: Mr Lemayian was looking older. Threads of silver now weaved through his red locs, and every motion of his limbs looked laboured. Had Mr Lemayian really lost his immortality?

Just as the question sprouted in his mind, a shout from Soni grabbed his attention. She and the others had the Shadow Queen surrounded in the centre of the room and Soni had just blasted a sonic wave into the core of her billowy form.

The Shadow Queen instantly split into three and Odwar watched in horror as separate white-eyed shadows formed out of each part of the triad. A bull, a beast and a boy, just as Mwikali had drawn.

Xirsi made a motion with his hands, as if directing aeroplane traffic, and the next minute a murder of crows blew through the shattered office windows. They flew straight into the shadow bull, encircling its head in a squawking mass of black feathery bodies. The bull

FIGHT VS. FREEZE

bucked and bellowed but couldn't escape the birds.

Mwikali brought her divining horn up to her puffed up cheeks and seemed to blow long and loud in the shadow boy's direction. One of the horn's magical properties must have been target precision because Odwar wasn't deafened by the loud sound this time. Nobody else in the room reacted to it either. Only the shadow boy collapsed onto the floor in pain.

Soni's sound blasts came hard and fast, striking the Shadow Queen with nonstop waves of sonic energy. The blows caused her to stagger backwards, farther and farther, until she was pinned against the wall.

The three shadows had been defeated. The battle had been won, or so it seemed. Until...

All it took was a glance for everything to change, an upwards flick of the Shadow Queen's head. And the moment her eyes locked on Odwar — up there, floating near the ceiling — the tide turned against the Intasimi Warriors.

The Shadow Queen squealed in delight, and all three shadows gained the strength they needed to rush up into the air at once, colliding, forming one large, roiling cloud of smoke. The cloud grew taller and spikier until it settled into its final form — that of the Shadow Queen. Only this time, she was bigger than ever.

She snaked around the room with a set of burning eyes, fixed solely on him. "Thank you my little shadow prince," she screeched.

Papers flew about in every direction as she circled, trapping everyone below her at the centre of a howling tornado.

Odwar watched helplessly as his friends held on tight to whatever they could find to keep from being whipped up into the air. Mr Lemayian clung to the handle of the trapdoor, while the others each gripped a leg of the office desk which, thankfully, was nailed to the floor.

"Odwar?" Soni shouted, noticing him for the first time. "What are you doing? You're making her stronger! You have to go back!"

Go back? Odwar's mind screamed against his rising panic. *Go back where?*

"Go back downstairs!" Xirsi commanded. "Get out of here! *NOW!*"

Odwar didn't want to believe that it was true. Had he really made the Shadow Queen stronger just by being there? Had he cost them the fight? Then something else occurred to him: how could he go back downstairs if he didn't know how he had gone upstairs in the first place?

The Shadow Queen laughed knowingly. "He can't do it! He doesn't know how. He doesn't know anything, really. He's no warrior. He's nothing but a scared...little... *boy!*"

Odwar's fury leapt to life at these words. He felt his little shadow begin to swell. Encouraged, he let the rage rip through his vapours. His shadow was growing, almost back to its regular size now — a small whirlwind, twisting against the ceiling.

Yes, his anger may have made the Shadow Queen stronger, but it made him stronger too. Maybe this time, it would even make him strong enough to defeat her all together.

Someone was yelling "Stop!" over and over again. Soni? Mwikali? It didn't matter. He ignored everything around him, focusing only on his fury, channelling it in torrents, until he felt like he could burst.

"Odwar! *Look!*"

The terror in Xirsi's voice somehow snapped him back to the present, and Odwar followed his friend's trembling finger to where it pointed, somewhere below him.

It took a moment for him to understand what he was looking at, but when he did, it made him numb with shock. His shadow was growing, yes, but it was also doing something far worse: it was bleeding into the Shadow Queen, becoming a part of her.

"It's too late!" she screeched victoriously. "It's already

done! I've already wo—"

All of a sudden, everything was gone and Odwar found himself downstairs in the basement office. He was back in his body, away from the Shadow Queen. He squinted the room into focus and saw Mr Lemayian standing in front of him, having snatched the fly whisk out of his hand. Then he heard Mwikali, Soni and Xirsi thundering down the stairs and watched as they staggered into the basement to join him.

His brain jogged to make sense of what had just happened. During the commotion, Mr Lemayian must have snuck back down into the basement and ripped the fly whisk out of his frozen hand. That's how he was able to return to his body and escape being swallowed up entirely by the Shadow Queen.

Odwar tried to open his mouth to speak but his lips wouldn't part. They were stuck together, sealed completely shut. Confused, he brought hands to his face and gasped when, instead of touching skin, his fingers sank into something soft and furry.

His heart pounded as he dug his nails in, pinched whatever it was off his face and raised his hands to his eyes.

The same substance that was caught between his fingers was covering his entire arm. In fact, when he looked down at himself, he found that it caked his chest and legs as well.

Every inch of him was covered in a thick, hairy layer of blackish green mould.

ODWAR VS. THE SHADOW QUEEN

Bull vs. Leopard

It took some time to scrape the mould off him. And even when most of it was cleared from his face, neck and hands, the rotten smell of fungus still filled his nostrils. Every breath reminded Odwar of what he had lost and what he was becoming.

Seated on the carpeted floor, slumped against one of the tall display shelves, he buried his face in his arms.

"Is it over?" he asked nobody in particular.

Silence filled the room downstairs, even while upstairs the raging winds continued. The Shadow Queen was still wreaking havoc above them.

"Doesn't sound like it. She's still up there," Soni said softly.

Tears burned at Odwar's throat as he lifted his eyes to meet his friends. "No, I mean, is the battle over? Did she win? Did *I* let her win?"

"If it was truly over, she wouldn't still be here," Mr Lemayian said, furiously clacking away at his laptop. He paused for a moment and looked over at Odwar, brows knitted. "If it was over, she'd be out in the world, riling up negative emotions and feeding off them. She'd be turning our world into the shadow world. But she's still here, which means she's still tethered to you. She can't leave. At least, not yet."

Sadness bubbled in Odwar's chest, surging up and finally clogging his throat, making his voice sound raspy and raw. "I'm sorry. I'm so sorry! I thought that if I could just be stronger than her, if I could just learn how to work my Entasim properly... Ugh, it's all my fault! If it wasn't for me, the Shadow Queen wouldn't even be here... in our world. *I* brought her here, *I* made her stronger. *I* did all of this!"

Mwikali slid onto the floor next to him and put a reassuring hand on his shoulder. "Remember last term when I got you suspended from school, but you gave me a second chance? You were able to look past what I did. It's my turn to do that for you too."

Soni and Xirsi slumped down beside them.

"You're always reminding me not to be too hard on myself," Soni said with a slight smile. "It's time to listen to your own advice. You were doing the best you could, Odwar. None of us blame you for any of this."

He shrugged her hand away and raised his trembling chin. "You *should* blame me. Mwikali's Entasim made her a better Seer, but mine? Mine has made me worse...

at everything! I've lost my shadow, my power… I've lost everything!"

Xirsi stood up, shaking his head. "That's not true! You haven't lost everything. You still have us."

Odwar could feel an overwhelming sadness uncoiling in his belly. "But without my superpower, I'm not an Intasimi Warrior. I'm nothing!"

A loud eruption rocked the room above them. The ceiling rumbled like thunder, the walls shook and the very air around them seemed to tremble.

Odwar froze, remembering that it was his emotions fuelling the Shadow Queen. He needed to calm down before he made things even worse.

But what could be worse than this?

An image of his father's rigid face popped into his mind. *That.* That would be worse than this. He could already hear Dad's voice ringing in his ears, telling him how disappointed he was, how it should have been Gor who was gifted with Intasimi powers.

He squeezed his eyes shut and fought to control his thoughts. But still, that disapproving baritone blared in Odwar's mind. It sounded all too loud… All too real…

"Son, open your eyes," the voice said. "It's me. Dad."

Odwar's eyelids snapped open and he staggered to his feet, because right there in front of him, was his father.

Dad's stern expression, striped suit and bright yellow tie filled the 55-inch screen that had come to life behind Mr Lemayian's desk.

It hadn't just been a voice in his head. His dad was there in the underground room, on video call. It must have been what Mr Lemayian was setting up on his laptop earlier.

Odwar neared the screen slowly, clenching his jaw in readiness for the mother — or father — of all lectures.

"I'm sorry," his father blurted out. Odwar stood slack-jawed, watching his father clear his throat. "I've been too tough on you...treating you the way my father treated me. I've not been fair. Your mum, your grandmother, Gor...they've helped me see that. I thought it would bring out the best in you...make you a stronger kid than I was. But instead, it's done the opposite. It's made you hate the best parts of yourself."

Odwar blinked in surprise. He had never heard his father sound like this — soft, gentle, caring. His usually tight jaw was replaced with a half-smile and instead of a fiery glare, it was warmth that glowed in his eyes.

"What I — we — love most about you," he said, motioning with his hand. He was soon joined on screen by two other people: Mum and Gor. They squeezed into the frame, smiling as Dad carried on. "What we all love about you is that you're loyal, loving and kind. We love that you make everyone around you feel seen and heard. On top of that, you're brave. You're always trying to protect others — your friends, nervous first-day-housekeepers who spill porridge...everyone! And that's exactly what a real warrior does: you think of others before yourself."

A sea of emotions crashed into Odwar. Tears swam in his eyes.

"I'm sorry I lied about my Entasim being at Kit-Mikayi," he choked out. "I just wanted to find it so badly... I thought it would make you proud of me. I thought it would make me a true warrior."

"You never needed the Entasim to make you strong, Odwar," his mother said with a gentle smile. "You've *always* been strong in the ways that matter most. You've always had the heart of a true warrior."

Grandmother's words echoed in his ears. *True power isn't just about strength. It's about compassion too. True power is about balance.*

His eyebrows flew up as meaning dawned on him. He had been so desperate to get stronger physically that he had been blinded to everything else — all the other things that made him a good warrior. And the harder he had tried to change who he was? The more *bad vibes* had been stirred up within him. His fly whisk had picked up on this dark energy, and amplified it, turning him into a shadow of himself — a raging bull-like shadow.

Doubt, however, still tugged at Odwar's heartstrings. "But what good am I if I can't even control my Entasim? If all I do is make the Shadow Queen stronger?"

Gor leaned forward with a smile. "You *can* control your Entasim, you big goof. All you need to do is remember everything that you already *are*. Draw that out. And don't let it turn you into someone you're not."

"Yeah, bro," Xirsi added, slapping his back. "You can do this." His crooked grin told Odwar that all was forgiven between them.

Mwikali took the fly whisk from Mr Lemayian's open hand and marched over to Odwar, pointing the object at his face. "This belongs to you. It'll make the *best* parts of you stronger. I just know it will."

"They're right," Mr Lemayian urged. "You can do this. You *can* master your Entasim. And you *can* defeat the Shadow Queen. As a team."

The room fell silent as they waited for Odwar to reclaim the orengo. It dangled from Mwikali's outstretched hand, its black hairs hovering in the air just in front of his nose. It was right there, the thing he had wanted so badly, the thing he had thought would solve all of his problems. His Entasim was right there within his reach.

But Odwar found that he couldn't move. He couldn't trust himself anymore. Not when he had lost control so many times and almost hurt others. Not when the fate of the world depended on it.

Mwikali sucked in a sharp breath, her face aglow with excitement. "Look!" Her eyeballs were roving all around him. "The dark haze around you...it's gone! The mould too!"

Odwar dropped his eyes to his shoes, then quickly searched the rest of his body. It was true! The fuzzy rot had completely gone, along with its smell. But that wasn't all. He *felt* different too — calmer, lighter, more like himself.

"And listen!" Xirsi exclaimed, his finger pointing up. The chaos above them was on the wane, confirming what he was saying, what Odwar himself felt — as his bad vibes faded, the Shadow Queen grew weaker.

Mwikali wiggled the fly whisk closer to his nose, and this time Odwar grabbed it. He rolled the handle in his palm slowly, feeling the familiar surge of strength spread through him once more. He even felt his skin heat up as blood pumped faster through his veins. But this time, instead of hate or anger, a quiet knowing wrapped itself around him.

True power was about what was on the inside, not outside.

He had been strong all along.

He closed his fingers around the fly whisk and raised it into the air. Despite the absence of daylight in the underground room, a twisting shadow appeared beside him. It jerked and jolted, bending from one shape to the other — first boy, then bull, then back to formless shadow.

Finally, it relaxed and began to swirl gently around him. Odwar closed his eyes, feeling calm, confident. He started to remember who he was, and what kind of a warrior he really wanted to be.

When his shadow finally settled into itself, it was in the form of a leopard. Its large, cat-like body stood waist-height by his side, with dark hollowed-out spots faintly visible against blackish grey fur.

Odwar couldn't help but smile as he looked at his shadow leopard — it was majestic, controlled, focused. His Entasim had done it! It had strengthened the best parts of him. He felt strong, but not in the kind of way that made him want to hurt and destroy — in a way that made him want to protect and defend.

Just like the leopard in his grandmother's story,

he felt poised and powerful with an equal measure of compassion too.

Odwar turned to the rest of the Intasimi Warriors with a renewed fire burning in his chest. "We're going back upstairs to stop the Shadow Queen once and for all."

ODWAR VS. THE SHADOW QUEEN

The Team vs. the Queen

They were winning at first. All four of them, using their unique powers to battle the Shadow Queen.

The Intasimi Warriors had burst out of the trapdoor like stampeding wildebeest. Mwikali blew her divining horn, Odwar's shadow leopard pounced, Soni blasted sound waves, and Xirsi summoned his wild kingdom.

The Shadow Queen was caught off guard. She hadn't expected them to recover that fast, or to be that strong and coordinated. Her shadow twisted, shrank, scattered, then came back together only to be ripped apart again. Every time she would lunge for one warrior, the other would come to their defence. The united team of four bolstered each other's strengths while diminishing their weaknesses, resulting in a convincing victory. *Almost.*

"You're still just a little boy!" the Shadow Queen screamed, trying to stoke Odwar's rage. "You'll never be anything but a little boy!"

This time, Odwar knew exactly what she was trying to do: weaken the team through him. But he wasn't going to fall for it. And so, with cool confidence, he pumped his

Entasim into the air, choosing to focus on their mission instead of the Shadow Queen's words.

Then, everything changed.

It started with a spine-chilling wail that sounded as if a cat, a bear and a monkey had all cried out at once. Next, a series of howls. And finally, the sound of jubilant laughter as the Shadow Queen cloned herself into two, then three, then dozens of mushrooming clouds. They shrieked with delight as they multiplied and cloaked the room in darkness.

All of a sudden, the Intasimi Warriors were up against a horde of shiny-eyed, vicious shadow spawn.

The four friends redoubled their efforts but their powers seemed useless against the blue-black swarm of creatures. As soon as they vanquished one, two more would spring up, multiplying over and over again, until only a tight space in the centre of the room was left unoccupied. It was here that the warriors formed a back-to-back huddle.

And just when it seemed like things couldn't get any worse, someone yelled out for help. It was Mr Lemayian. The shadow spawn had him strung up mid-air, leaving him dangling by his feet.

A bolt of panic slammed into Odwar. Mr Lemayian was trapped, completely helpless against the throng of creatures surrounding him. His locs looked even greyer now, his body thinner than it had looked before. Could he have aged several more years in just a few minutes? Odwar shelved the thought at the back of his mind. Right now, all that mattered was saving him.

Without hesitation, he broke out of the cluster and sprinted towards his mentor. His shadow leopard bounded ahead, knocking shadow spawn out of its way as it tore across the room.

It was only when he skidded to a stop just below Mr Lemayian, and looked back at his friends, that he realised his mistake.

He had left a hole in the armour of their team huddle, a gaping space where he should have remained, where a throng of spawn now streamed in. One by one, the creatures overpowered his friends and hoisted them up into the air. Mwikali, Soni and Xirsi kicked and screamed, tried to use their powers, but it was no use. In mere seconds, they were wrapped like mummies in blankets of shadow and pasted flat against the ceiling.

Odwar froze in horror. Somewhere behind him, the Shadow Queen's devilish laugh rang out, but he could scarcely hear it above the rushing sound filling his ears. Her laughter grew alongside his fear, and he could sense her knitting herself back together, growing bigger and stronger by the second.

Odwar couldn't move. Couldn't think. Couldn't even breathe.

"It's almost over little shadow prince," she sang wickedly.

She reared up in front of him then, gorging on shadow creatures and swallowing them up to make herself larger than ever. So large that she covered up the ceiling and his friends along with it.

A pained yowl from below made Odwar turn. His shadow leopard was being dragged along the floor by two long shadowy arms. The Shadow Queen looked like she was playing tug of war, pulling his leopard hand over fist into her massive form.

Odwar drove his fly whisk into the air, even jumped up and down, but nothing could stop what was happening. She was already too strong. Within seconds, his shadow leopard was gone, gobbled up into her like the rest of the shadow beings.

"It's over!" she growled. "I'm FREE!"

A bang.

A chorus of other-worldly wails.

A squeal of laughter.

Then, spawn shooting out of their queen, out of the windows, and straight into the world, with the Shadow

Queen flying out right behind them.

Odwar squeezed himself into a corner and watched the nightmare unfold. It was over. The Shadow Queen was untethered — free to turn earth into a realm of shadows, darkness and despair. He had failed his friends, family, and the entire world. He wasn't the warrior they all believed him to be. What good was inner strength if it couldn't save the world from evil?

As the Shadow Queen whizzed around the quad and then out onto the field, gloating in her victory, setting free more creatures from the shadow world, Odwar clung to his father's kind words.

What we love about you is that you're loyal, loving and kind. We love that you make everyone around you feel seen and heard.

You make everyone around you feel seen and heard. Seen…and…heard.

An idea sparked. A flare of hope. A last-ditch chance to stop the world from descending into chaos.

He pushed himself off the ground and placed one shaky foot in front of the other.

If true power was the balance of strength and compassion, if bad energy fuelled the Shadow Queen, if sometimes the best thing you could do for a person was to make them feel seen and heard, then that was exactly what he was going to do.

He was going to fight evil with kindness, to push back darkness with light.

He kept walking, stopping a few inches away from the Shadow Queen. There, he took a final sharp breath. And then, he leaped into her.

Right into the belly of the beast.

*

A sea of twisting black winds immediately swallowed him up.

"Show me!" Odwar begged. "Please! Show me what happened to you!"

A column of air rushed at him in response, rumbling and rotating violently.

For a split second, he feared that this plan would fail, but for the sake of the world and all those he loved in it, he tried again. "That was you in the vision, wasn't it? The young woman? The one who was carried away by those men? That was *you*."

The spiralling winds slowed and hushed.

Encouraged, he pushed on. "I'd like to know what happened. I know the legend that's been taught to me all my life, but now I want to hear *your* side of the story.

Please. I'm listening."

In an instant, everything stilled. Silence boomed in the vacuum as Odwar held his breath. Then, after what seemed like a lifetime but was only a few minutes, a shoreline, lake and queue of busy fishing canoes started to take form in the distance.

Relief shuddered through him upon recognising the familiar scene. And this time, he was ready when the young woman appeared. As before, she ran along the beach and into the arms of the man she loved, throwing her head back in delight when they embraced. As always, when her face sparkled with joy, Odwar felt happiness fill him up too.

When the gang of men showed up, his body tightened. He watched them glide across the sand like a wave of angry crabs. And even though he had watched it happen many times before, his anger flared when they grabbed the woman by the waist and whisked her away. He dug his fingernails into his thighs as he watched her claw at her kidnapper's back. A scream tore from his throat when she cried for them to stop hurting the young man.

Everything in the vision happened exactly as it had before, but right before the scene cut, something unexpected happened. The Shadow Queen spoke.

She didn't scream, didn't taunt, didn't mock. She

spoke to him. And when she did, her voice was sad and soft.

When she did, it was to tell him her side of the story...

Woman vs. Monster

That was my last taste of happiness on earth. That was the day my life ended.

They took me away from the only one I had ever loved, dragged me away from everything I had ever known. They needed me for their plan. I was someone they could use. Someone nobody would miss — an orphan, with no family left in the world.

The day they took me, they told me that my life would only serve one purpose from then on: to become Lwanda Magere's second wife. I no longer belonged to myself. I no longer had any other name. From then on, I was to be known only as the Second Wife.

My mission was to find out Lwanda's secret — what made him invincible — so that the warriors from my village could finally defeat him in battle.

I begged them to let me go back to the one I loved, but...it was no use. They banished him from our village forever, told me to forget about him, said I no longer had a future except the one they had plotted for me.

I tried to run away before my Ayie ceremony when the

groom asks for the bride's hand in marriage. Funny, Ayie means "I agree", but nobody cared to ask if I agreed. If they had, I would have told them that I didn't. I wanted to have my own life, my own future.

They caught me sneaking out in the middle of the night as I tried to escape and they...they punished me. They made me understand that I was going to become the Second Wife, whether I liked it or not.

The Shadow Queen didn't just tell Odwar what happened, she showed him too. Against a shadowy backdrop, he watched a brood of traditionally-dressed women bustle around the young woman. Celebratory horns and lively stringed instruments played in the background, signalling the start of a special occasion — it was the day of the Ayie ceremony.

The women clucked excitedly as they fixed the last piece of decoration on the new bride's head: a string of white beads. But while they laughed, she cried. Rivers of tears gushed out of bruised eyes and flowed down her puffy cheeks.

Nobody seemed to care — not as she wept, not even when she stumbled on her way out of the hut. They had pushed a platter of food into the young woman's hands and shoved her forwards, ordering her to serve her husband-to-be. She didn't dare fall for she would have been made to pay severely if she had. The large mound of stiff maize flour porridge — ugali — with a side of stewed chicken and smoked beef that she carried thankfully remained intact.

Tears stung Odwar's eyes as he watched her limp forwards. And when she arrived at a cluster of men squatting on short three-legged stools, he gasped in spite of himself as one of them stood up to greet her. He knew instantly who this man was — it was the young woman's husband to be, the legendary warrior, his invincible Intasimi ancestor.

It was Lwanda Magere.

He was built like a superhero action figure: impossibly tall, with a chest that stretched for miles and muscles chiselled like concrete blocks. An apron made of dark brown animal hide hung from his waist, and atop his head he wore an enormous headdress of animal fur and ostrich plumes. He held a tall wooden spear in one hand and…no shield in the other.

Of course! Odwar thought excitedly. Lwanda Magere didn't carry a shield because he was invincible! Nothing could break through his rock-like skin. Next Mashujaa Day, Odwar vowed to leave the shield out of his traditional dress-up costume. If there *was* a next

Mashujaa Day. Odwar shuddered at the thought.

The larger-than-life warrior smiled and extended a hand to greet the young woman. Glistening white teeth sparkled against shiny black skin on a face that bore no signs of his age. While his top row of teeth was perfectly intact, his lower row was missing six whole teeth. Like all Luo men, Lwanda Magere had undergone a painful tooth extraction as a boy to mark his initiation into adulthood. Nevertheless, his broad, gappy smile reached all the way to his eyes.

It faltered when the woman turned away from him. Lwanda looked to the men surrounding him with concern, asking them without words if something was wrong. Odwar recognised some of them from the vision. These were the same men who had kidnapped the young woman. Lwanda Magere had no idea that she had been forced to marry him or that she was on a mission to betray him.

One of the men smiled calmly at Lwanda and then, behind his back, narrowed his eyes in warning at the young woman. She flinched in alarm and then strained her face into a smile before presenting her new husband with his meal.

I needed to play the role of Second Wife perfectly for their plan to work — their plan to kill Lwanda Magere. My people, the Lang'o, had been in conflict with his people, the Luo, for generations. But we could never get the upper hand over them, not when they had the invincible Lwanda Magere on their side.

So they presented me as a peace offering to Lwanda, and convinced his people that this was the only way our two communities could live in harmony. In truth, I was a virus sent to burrow inside the enemy's walls and infect them from within.

As Second Wife, I was able to get close to him and find out what the secret to his strength really was. I was able to provide the key to defeating the Luo once and for all.

After the Ayie ceremony, I moved into my new home, and over time, I convinced myself that once my mission was complete, the elders would let me go back to my own life. I told myself that all I needed to do was this one thing — find out Lwanda Magere's secret — and then I would finally be free.

I got my chance not long after our ceremony, while his first wife, Mikayi, was away and I was the only one left behind to look after him, when he fell terribly ill...

Lwanda Magere lay on a small wooden cot, his body shivering beneath the cover of cow hide. He seemed to doze in and out of sickly sleep as the young woman rearranged wood on a fire that burned next to him.

She watched him carefully for a while before slowly approaching the cot with a calabash bowl filled with green paste — herbal medicine meant to be rubbed on the skin.

Odwar's heart was pounding so hard that he could feel it in his ears. This story had been told to him for as long as he could remember, and now he was about to watch everything happen with his very own eyes.

The young woman slowly lifted the animal skin, exposing muscles that, though smaller than before, still bulged more than most. She scooped up the paste with her fingers and rubbed it in her palms before reaching for his chest.

She was inches away from Lwanda's skin when he suddenly jerked awake and grabbed her tiny hands with just one of his. His eyes blazed with suspicion as they bore into her. Hers rounded in fear as they stared back at him.

For a few tense seconds they remained like this, her face scrunching in pain as he seemed to tighten his grip on her. Slowly, he reached behind him with his other hand and pulled out a knife.

Odwar could hardly breathe. This was it. This was the moment Lwanda Magere's tragic fate was sealed.

Gently, he squeezed the knife into her palms. He then pointed at the ground, at his shadow, but she shook her head, confused. So he made a cutting motion and then pointed at it again.

The young woman nodded, finally understanding, and then crouched down on the floor. After one last look at him to be sure, she dragged the blade across his shadow where he had instructed and then slumped back in surprise.

Bright red blood was bubbling up from the soil, spilling from the line the knife had drawn. Lwanda Magere's shadow was bleeding.

He nudged her a few times with the bowl of herbs, finally managing to draw her startled eyes away from his oozing shadow. When he had her full attention, he pointed at the cut on the ground then at the sticky, green paste.

She understood what he was saying. She understood everything. He wanted her to smear the medicine on his shadow. Because that was where his power rested. *That* was the secret to his strength.

His shadow.

I went straight to the elders that night and told them everything. I begged them to let me go since I had done all they had asked. But they refused, told me to wait until after Lwanda Magere was fully defeated. Then, they would free me, take me back to the village with them, allow me to go back to my own life.

The Lang'o warriors attacked a day later in an ambush that the Luo never saw coming. Why would they? The two communities were supposed to be at peace!

It was no matter though, the Luo weren't afraid. They had the invincible warrior, Lwanda Magere, on their side. Nobody could defeat them.

At first they couldn't understand why all Lang'o spears were being spiked at the ground. But when one of those spears pierced Lwanda's shadow and he fell to his knees, they realised what had happened. The enemy had found out his secret.

I watched in horror as my people fled in victory, leaving me behind. They didn't so much as spare me a look. They had never meant to free me. I was always going to be a sacrifice to their cause.

I knew then that I would never be free.

I still remember the hurt in Lwanda Magere's eyes as he drew his last breath, right before his body folded and hardened into a rock. He searched the village square for me and pointed a damning finger in my direction. He was letting everyone know who it was that had betrayed him.

After that, well... You know what happened after that.

The vision and everyone in it dissolved into violently spinning dark vapours and Odwar was left standing alone once again at the epicentre of the Shadow Queen's rage.

"I was the one who was betrayed!" she screamed wildly. "They took everything away from me, forced me to do what they wanted, and then...abandoned me. Nobody cared about what I had lost, who I was before they took me, before—"

"I care! Tell *me* who you are," Odwar shouted above the windstorm.

"Wh— What?" She stammered. "You know who I am."

"No! Tell me who you *really* are," Odwar stressed, saying it slowly so she understood his true meaning. "You're not a monster. We nicknamed you the Shadow Queen, but that isn't the real you...it's what *happened* to you. It's what they turned you into. Who were you before they took you, when you belonged to yourself? What was your name?"

Everything around him suddenly exploded into ear-splitting chaos. The edges of the tornado whipped faster, the winds howled louder, the ground beneath his feet threatened to crack wide open.

Odwar cupped his hands over his ears and bowed his

head, preparing himself for the worst. And just when he was sure the storm would tear him apart, it stopped, and the shadow world dropped into deathly silence.

He didn't dare breathe. And then...

"My name was... My name is Chepngetich," she said, her voice barely above a whisper.

"Chep-nge-teech," Odwar tried slowly. The "ng" part sounded a lot like the "ng" at the end of the words "singing" or "sleeping."

"My father said that my name reminded him of the best time of his childhood. When he was a young boy, his mother would take him with her to the lake in the morning. Nam Lolwe would be glimmering in the early light of dawn, and together they would sit on its shores, waiting for the fishermen to bring in the day's catch. The golden promise of a new day, the bubbly music of the lake weaving through the air, and the warmth of his mother beside him made him feel at peace with everything that was and was to come."

"Chepngetich — at peace," Odwar said softly. "My mother once told me that there's a world of meaning behind the names parents give their children."

And at the sound of those words, the dark cloud faded away to reveal a young woman. *The* young woman. She looked just as she had in the vision, before she was made the Second Wife, before she became the Shadow Queen.

"My name *is* Chepngetich," she repeated, her eyes glistening with tearful determination. "That is the name my parents gave me. That is who I am."

Suddenly feeling the fly whisk in his hand, and remembering what he had learnt from Mr Lemayian, Odwar slowly raised it and held it in the air. And when Chepngetich bowed her head in response, he waved it six times over her head. He said her name each time as he did so, showing her that she was seen, heard, *honoured*, for who she truly was.

Chepngetich's face gleamed as she looked back at Odwar. Then, right in front of him, she started to recede into the background. Every time he blinked, he re-opened his eyes to find that she had moved back another few yards. He raced forward trying to keep up with her but it was no use. With a blissful smile on her face, she was being drawn into the Mugumo Groves — the earthly dwelling place for the souls of the ancestors.

Just before she vanished into the thicket of trees completely, her eyes widened with a memory. "What's happening to your mentor," she shouted urgently, "the aging. It shouldn't be happening. Not this way. Someone is *making* it happen."

The hairs on Odwar's neck jumped up. "Who? Who's making it hap—"

He stopped short when he realised that he was back in Mr Lemayian's office, with his shadow leopard by his side and a ring of smiling friends all around him.

The Young vs. the Old

Odwar's father slapped the steering wheel and let out a hearty laugh. "So, let me get this straight. Not only is your shadow a leopard now, but it also has red spots, the same ones you now have on your head? And to top it all off, you got to see Lwanda Magere *and* Chepngetich in real space and time before she became the Shadow Queen?"

"Yup," Odwar beamed. "It was pretty wild. My leopard's spots aren't exactly like the ones in my hair though. His have a shimmer to them, like glow-in-the-dark stars, only they're bright red spots."

With his dad and mum in the front and him and Gor in the back, the family was driving away from Savanna Academy on their way to lunch with the rest of the Intasimi families. For once, there wasn't any tension in the air between him and his dad or between him and Gor. For the first time in a long time, Odwar felt like there was nothing separating him from the men in his family.

He leaned sideways to catch a glimpse of his newly

transformed hair in the car's rear view mirror. On the sides and back of his head, where his fade was cut low enough to see through to the scalp, red leopard-like spots were tattooed on his skin. According to his friends, they had popped up right before he woke from the shadow world.

If Odwar had had to guess, they had appeared on his head at the exact same time he was waving the fly whisk over Chepngetich. Acts of honour and valour like those were usually rewarded by the ancestors with red hair — a distinguishing feature of true warriors of the past. Mwikali's hair had also received its red streaks after a similar act of bravery and kindness. Apparently, she had jumped into the air when Odwar's red spots had emerged, excited that another member of the team had a matching colour in their hair.

Gor nodded at the new hairdo approvingly and punched Odwar playfully in the arm. "Like I said, you were born to do this."

"Agreed," Dad said with an adoring gaze. "I'm proud of what you did back there."

"We all are," Mum joined in, with her phone to her ear. "Including your grandmother. She says to tell you good job and to ask if you 'finally understand that you were the leopard in the story and she always knew you would earn your spots by showing compassion to the snake'... Do you have any idea what that means?" Mum's eyebrows looked puzzled as she lowered the phone and turned to Odwar.

He smiled. "Yeah. Tell her that I understand. There's a lot more to being a warrior than strength — it's about who you are on the inside and how you treat other people too. True strength comes from the heart."

*

"De-li-cious!" Xirsi sang, licking his fingertips. He had just inhaled another one of Soni's dad's famous barbecued ribs.

"Your dad's nyama choma is elite!" Mwikali praised in between bites.

Soni flashed her usual proud smile and nodded. Her friends said the same thing every time they came over to her place.

Just about every weekend since their powers had revealed themselves, the Intasimi Warriors and their families had met together for a shared meal. And after several hours spent cleaning up Mr Lemayian's office, all had readily accepted the invitation to Soni's house for a picnic lunch.

As soon as they could throw a Maasai blanket onto the backyard grass, the four friends were spread out on it, savouring the smells of roasting meat as the mellow tunes of Kenyan singer, Karun, played in the background.

Odwar snuck a glance at the parents huddled around the charcoal grill, before leaning in to his friends. "Are we going to say anything to Mr Lemayian?" he whispered. "You know...about what Chepngetich said?"

"Maybe he already knows," Mwikali said. "The question is, who's doing it? Who's making him lose his immortality?"

"To start with, I was never actually immortal," a deep voice announced.

Mr Lemayian had suddenly popped up behind them. He had a knack for creeping up without a sound, and it startled them every time.

"There's a difference between being immortal and being long-lived," he explained matter-of-factly, as he lowered himself slowly onto the grass next to them.

Xirsi put a finger on his chin. "Yeah, I've read about that. Unlike immortals, long-lived people actually *do* age, they just do it really slowly."

Mr Lemayian nodded. "Exactly. I was never meant to live forever, just for a really long time."

"But Chepngetich told Odwar that someone was doing this to you. Someone is making you age a lot faster than you should," Soni said, eyebrows furrowed.

"I'm afraid so. And I fear that it has something to do with the underworld. I'm afraid we might be dealing with a Life Drinker — a creature that sucks the life-force from others to gain immortality."

A stunned silence filled the space between the warriors as Mr Lemayian's words sunk in. None of them could imagine a life without the help and guidance of their mentor. It was the one way the monsters of the underworld could hurt them the most, without actually having to fight them.

"How... How much time do you have left?" Odwar asked, almost choking on the words.

Mr Lemayian pinched the bridge of his nose and shook his head slowly. "I don't quite know. Years, maybe months."

"*What*? We're *not* going to let that happen," Soni vowed, sticking her nose in the air. "We're going to find this life sucker person and we're going to stop them."

"It's Life *Drinker*," Mr Lemayian said with a chuckle. "And no, you can't get involved. The council doesn't want you to. This is my problem, and I'll figure it out. Don't worry about it."

The council of elders was made up of the parents of the Intasimi Warriors. They had always been antsy about their kids fighting evil. Even though they were the parents of specially gifted children and part of a supernatural council, at the end of the day they were just that — parents. And they tried to do what parents always do: keep their kids out of harm's way.

"But we're so much better at using our powers now... We can do this! Let us help you!" Soni pleaded.

Mr Lemayian planted his palms on the grass and slowly cranked himself up into a standing position. Only days before, he would have jumped off the ground in one quick move. Now, his knees popped like firecrackers as he struggled to pull himself up.

"We — the council — have made up our minds and it's not up for discussion," he said when he was finally upright. "You kids just enjoy the barbecue. You did well today, just like I knew you would."

Odwar stared in disbelief at Mr Lemayian as he hobbled away. "So that's it? We're just supposed to sit back and do nothing?"

Mwikali and Xirsi sighed and shook their heads, too bewildered to speak. Soni, meanwhile, didn't seem to have heard a word he said. With her lips pursed and eyes squinted, she was clicking furiously on her phone.

Odwar snapped his fingers impatiently in front of her. "Hello? Earth to Soni? I said, are we just going to let Mr Lemayian go out like this?"

Soni shoved his hand aside and sat up. Still staring intently into her phone she spoke in a near-whisper. "Life Drinker: a creature that maintains immortality by feeding on the life energy of its victims. Also called energy vampire, these beings drain the life of unsuspecting individuals, causing them to grow older. Powerful life drinkers can consume the entire life force of their victims in a matter of..."

Soni's wide eyes flicked up to meet Odwar's. Her bottom lip trembled as her breathing turned into short, shallow pants.

Gently, Odwar pried the phone away from her stiff fingers and continued reading from the monster encyclopedia page. "Powerful life drinkers can consume the entire life force of their victims in a matter of...*weeks*."

"Weeks?" Mwikali shrieked.

Xirsi grabbed both sides of his curly head. "This is bad. This is *soooo* bad!"

Odwar's nose started to sting. "You mean, in just a few weeks, Mr Lemayian could be...could be..."

"NO!" Soni gritted out, snatching her phone back and shoving it inside her pocket. "Nothing is going to happen to Mr Lemayian. Because we're going to find the Life Drinker and put a stop to him...her...it! And we're going to do it whether the council likes it or not."

She looked at each of her friends' faces, knowing their answer even before she asked the question: "Who's with me?"

The End

Acknowledgements

I thank and praise you, God of my ancestors: you have shown me grace, given me wisdom and bestowed on me power.

About the author

Shiko Nguru was born and raised in Nairobi, the bustling capital city of Kenya. After a childhood spent climbing trees to find perfect perches to read books in, she spent her formative years in the United States, where she discovered just how cold a Midwestern winter could be and how much one person could miss the smell of freshly fried mandazis.

By the time she returned to Kenya, Shiko was sure of two things: that she was ready to spend the rest of her life in her homeland, and that she wanted to dedicate that life to telling her people's stories. The idea for the Intasimi Warriors series was born out of her love of African mythology, and the realisation that precious few books featured characters that looked like her or her children.

Intasimi means "magical charm" in the Maa language of the Maasai people, and captures perfectly how enchanting she believes the people of East Africa's stories to be. She delights in bringing African history to life and looks forward to telling more stories filled with fun, magic and adventure...

About the cover artist

Melissa McIndoe is an artist currently based in upstate New York. Her professional work includes children's book illustrations for small publishing houses and independent creators. She has also made storyboards for animation. In her free time, Melissa enjoys spending time with her dog, hiking up mountains and drawing comics. Oh, and tea. Lots of tea.

The Intasimi Warriors Series
by Shiko Nguru

Set in modern-day Nairobi, Kenya, this thrilling series follows four young friends as they learn to wield their new-found powers as the descendants of the Intasimi: an ancient bloodline of legendary East African warriors. Follow Mwikali, Odwar, Soni and Xirsi as they race against time to learn how to channel their ancestors' powers while pitting themselves against a terrifying array of malign forces that are intent on using dark magic to destroy everything the friends hold dear. Inspired by the author's Kenyan heritage, this fast-paced, action-packed series is bursting with East African mythology and gripping to the very end.

The Bollywood Academy Series
by Puneet Bhandal

Set in Mumbai, India, this dazzling school series, packed with endearing characters, true-to-life relationships and authentic cultural details, charts the fortunes of students at the city's most prestigious stage school. Home to future film stars and movie producers, the Bollywood Academy sets the stage for the students to make friends, break friends, plot revenge and most importantly dream big as they prepare for life on — or off — the silver screen. Full of stylish outfits, fabulous film shoots, and one too many brushes with the paparazzi, this series is as glamorous as its star-studded cast.

In case you missed it...

An Extract from
Mwikali and the Forbidden Mask
Book 1 of the Intasimi Warriors series

The ~~Freak~~ Chameleon

You can hide a lot behind a smile. And as Mwikali stood in front of the mirror that morning, she practised all the different types of smiles she could think of.

The first smile made her look overly excited and far too eager, like a puppy panting for a frisbee. The next was impossibly sweet and wide-eyed in a way that made her look half-crazy. And the last smile was so tight and forced that she might as well have been holding a neon sign above her head letting everyone know she was hiding something.

None of the smiles were believable. So, Mwikali dropped the corners of her mouth and took in a deep breath. *Plan B: no smile.* Instead, she would try not to be seen at all. Her new plan was to be the unsmiling, plain, ordinary girl who nobody noticed. She was going to fade into the background. Be invisible. Disappear. It was the only way to make sure nobody discovered the truth about her.

"Mwikali!" Her mum's voice rang out from outside her bedroom. "Hurry up or you'll miss the minibus!"

Mwikali scooped up the backpack resting at her feet. "I'll be right there!" she yelled, before turning back to the mirror.

Scanning her reflection, she smoothed down her school uniform for the umpteenth time. The girl in the mirror looked as normal as could be. She had the height of a normal twelve year old. Wore a normal uniform — white blouse, red tie, blue skirt with a matching jumper. And even though her almond-shaped eyes were larger than most, they were perfectly suited to her deep brown face.

Mwikali grabbed a hair band and tied her thick, jet-black Afro into a ponytail, making sure she rounded out and tucked in all the loose ends, forming a tight bun on top of her head. Her scalp ached in protest but Mwikali pushed through the discomfort. As much as she loved her loose, fluffy hair, it had to remain hidden away. The plan was to be as unnoticeable as possible.

She clenched and unclenched her hands, worry clouding her face. Everything about the girl in the mirror looked normal, but deep down she knew that she wasn't normal at all.

I'm a freak. A dangerous, very not-normal freak.

The memory of names others had called her brought a familiar tightness to Mwikali's chest. She crumpled handfuls of skirt in her clammy hands as her heart began to thump.

Stop this! she commanded herself. She couldn't lose it. Not today. She wanted today to go well. *Needed* it to go well. Today was her first day at a new school. It was a chance to start afresh. A chance to leave behind all the horrible things that had happened at her last school. For that to happen, she needed to act normal. Boring even. She had to hide who she really was.

"Haraka, haraka, Mwikali!" Mum called out, more urgently than before. "Hurry up or you'll be late!"

With one last glance at the mirror, Mwikali exhaled sharply and then swung her bedroom door open. "Coming!"

Continued in
Mwikali and the Forbidden Mask (2022)